DREAMWORKS
SHREK
THE THIRD

DREAMWORKS

SHREK THE THIRD™

THE JUNIOR NOVEL

Adapted by

Kathleen Weidner Zoehfeld

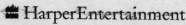

HarperEntertainment

An Imprint of HarperCollinsPublishers

Chapter One

Prince Charming galloped across the open plain on Chauncey, his trusty steed. The horse's golden mane flew in the wind. Lightning flashed in the sky and thunder rumbled and rolled.

"Onward, Chauncey, to the highest room of the tallest tower!" cried Prince Charming valiantly. "My princess awaits rescue by her handsome prince."

The spotlights were on in a little run-down theater on the outskirts of the fabled land of Far Far Away. Charming was playing his part with gusto, but the audience grumbled and fidgeted in their seats. As soon as the curtain had gone

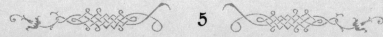 

up, they'd realized they were in for a low-budget produc-tion. The prince's "steed" was just a wooden hobbyhorse. And the set was even worse! A wobbly castle tower sat in front of the cheaply painted backdrop.

Prince Charming pretend-galloped up to the base of the tower.

"Whoa there, Chauncey!" he cried. He dismounted, tossed his blond hair back with a flourish, and set his stick horse down on the stage.

A princess leaned out of the tower window. "Hark!" she cried. "The brave Prince Charming approacheth."

"Fear not, fair maiden!" cried Charming. "I shall slay the monster that guards you and then take my place as rightful king."

A short, round actor in a cheap ogre costume shuffled onto the stage. *"Grrrrrrrrr!"* he cried.

The audience cheered.

Prince Charming glanced out at the audience in disbe-lief. Why were they cheering for the ogre!? He HATED that ogre. And everyone else should hate him, too!

Charming pulled himself together and struggled to

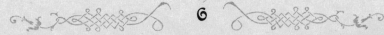

remember his words. "Prepare, foul beast, to enter into a world of pain with which you are not familiar!"

A heckler in the audience stood up and tossed his chair. "Off the stage, Goldilocks!" he jeered. Charming ducked as the chair whizzed past him. He watched it slide across the stage and bump into the rickety tower.

He cleared his throat nervously. "Prepare, foul beast . . ."

The tower creaked and groaned behind him. He glanced over his shoulder and cringed. The whole stage set was about to collapse!

The backdrop came down around him with a loud boom.

Prince Charming stood amid the rubble, without a scratch. He was covered with dust, his feet perfectly framed by the princess's window.

The ogre and the audience roared with laughter.

Furious, Prince Charming shook his mangled sword at them all. "Someday you'll be sorry!"

"We already are!" joked another heckler.

Charming threw down his sword, picked up his horse, and stalked off the stage. He stepped outside into the dark

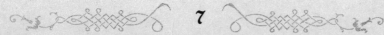

alley, where he had set up a makeshift dressing room for himself. On the hill in the distance he could see the towers of the magnificent castle of Far Far Away. He remembered that horrible ogre, Shrek, and how he had robbed him of his chance to rule the land. Prince Charming sat down at his broken vanity and sobbed.

When he finally looked up, the picture of his Fairy Godmother taped to his vanity mirror caught his eye. In her handwriting across the bottom it said: "Don't stop believing! Mommy's little angel."

Prince Charming sighed. "You're right, mother. I can't let this happen. I can't!"

He stood up, threw his shoulders back, and fixed the castle in his steely gaze. He held his chin up high. "I am the rightful king of Far Far Away," he cried, "and I promise you this, Mother. I will restore dignity to my throne!"

At that moment a gust of wind blew a newspaper right into his face. He peeled it off and looked at it. Splashed across the front page was a picture of Shrek and his new bride, Princess Fiona, waving regally to a crowd of citizens. That was wrong, wrong, wrong! It was he, Prince

Charming, who should be married to the princess. That's the way the story was *supposed* to go!

"This time, no one will stand in my way!" he shouted, crumpling the paper up into a tight ball. "NO ONE!"

Chapter Two

Meanwhile, at the castle, Shrek and Fiona were having trouble adjusting to the royal routine. They awoke to the sun shining through their bedroom window. But they had only the briefest moment to gaze at each other fondly and say good morning when Donkey popped up, bright and chipper, beside their bed.

"*Good morning!*" he sang.

Puss In Boots wasn't far behind. He popped his head through the cat flap. "Good morning!"

Donkey continued his cheery song. "*The sun is*

shining through. Good morning. Good morning to you. And you."

"And you," added Puss.

"And yooooooooou . . ." Donkey serenaded in Shrek's ear.

Shrek put his ogre hands around Donkey's muzzle and looked him in the eye. "Ha, ha. That was great," he said. "Now do you know the little ditty about the ogre that skinned the donkey?"

Shrek pointed to the door meaningfully.

"Yeah, yeah, sleepyhead," said Donkey, ignoring him. "It's time to clock in. And as usual, your executive administrative assistants are here to make sure all your appointments go as royal as jelly."

"Si," added Puss. "You have a very full day filling in for the king and queen. There are several functions that require your attendance, sir."

"Oh joy," Shrek sighed.

"Now let's get a move on!" cried Donkey.

He yanked the sheets off Shrek's bed and gasped at

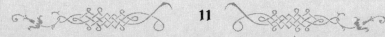

the sight of the ogre's bare legs. *"Aaaahhhh!"* he cried. "You know, you really need to get yourself a pair of jammies."

What could Shrek do!? His old friend, Donkey, was right. Like it or not, there was work to be done. With Fiona's father turned into a frog now and sick in bed, it was up to Shrek to look after the kingly duties.

The first thing on the schedule was a knighting ceremony. Shrek braced himself and walked down the aisle of the crowded church. The young soldier who was due to be knighted that day looked on nervously as Shrek approached. This was not exactly the king he had expected!

Puss bowed and handed Shrek a sword. With his own sword Puss demonstrated how a knighting was done— one light touch of the sword on each of the soldier's shoulders.

Shrek practiced—one touch here, one there. Shrek looked over his shoulder at Puss to make sure he was doing it right, when all of a sudden, he accidentally stabbed the knight!

 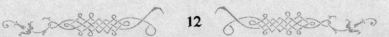

The crowd gasped in horror.

"Ewwww!" cried Donkey.

Shrek didn't know what to do! All day long, things went from bad to worse. Once they'd gotten help for the poor soldier, it was time to attend a christening ceremony for a new boat in the Royal Navy. This didn't go any better. The admiral handed Shrek the bottle of champagne for the christening. Shrek leaned against the ship for just a second—and the ship started to sail away. In a panic to smash the bottle against the ship, as was the custom in Far Far Away, Shrek threw the bottle at the ship with his mighty ogre arm. The bottle smashed a hole in the side of the ship, and the whole thing sank like a stone.

Donkey and Puss looked at each other in dismay.

A crowd of citizens was gathering, and they didn't look happy.

Finally, the royal ball was scheduled for the evening, and Shrek's executive administrative assistants decided it was time to haul him off to Raul for a serious makeover.

Raul, the royal makeup artist, tied aprons around Shrek and Fiona and scrutinized the big, green ogres.

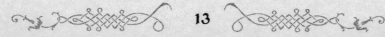

"We've had a tough run," declared Donkey, "but that's all gonna change at tonight's mixer. We are gonna make sure you look your best."

"Can you make your magic work for us, Raul?" asked Puss.

"I will see what I can do," replied Raul.

He opened up a bag full of gardening tools.

Shrek raised an eyebrow. What kind of makeover would it take for him to look even remotely like a king?

Raul hauled out a circular sander and began filing down Shrek's gruesome toenails.

Next it was time for makeup. A tear welled up in Shrek's ogre eye as Raul applied mascara. Could being king possibly be worth all this trouble?

Fiona wasn't any happier. She was in the next chair, having her nose hairs plucked.

"*Ow!*" she cried.

Then, lipstick for both. Stylish clothes. Socks and tight little shoes. Collars and corsets and rivets and belts . . . !

Finally, the new royal couple, trimmed and painted and cinched, stood before Donkey and Puss, all decked out in

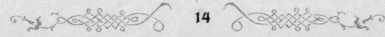

the finest Renaissance regalia.

Donkey and Puss gasped with delight at what they saw.

"Uh, is this really necessary?" asked Fiona.

"Ho, ho. Quite necessary, Fiona," said Raul to Shrek.

"I'm SHREK, you twit," cried Shrek.

"Whatever," said Raul.

"Okay, peoples!" cried Puss. "This isn't a rehearsal. Let's see some hustle." The ball was about to begin.

"Smiles, everyone! Smiles!" coached Donkey.

The royal page began to announce the guests as they arrived:

". . . The Duke and Duchess of Cheesington . . . Lord Meatballs and Lady Redsauce . . . Lord Kooser and Lady Luncheonmeat . . . Master Wooten and Lady Beshears . . ."

Shrek took Fiona's hand. "I don't know how much longer I can keep this up." He sighed.

"Just grin and bear it, okay? It's just until Dad gets better," said Fiona.

She paused a moment. "Shrek?"

"Yeah?"

She smiled. "You look handsome."

Shrek relaxed a little and smiled back.

Fiona puckered her lips, and Shrek leaned in for a kiss. But, alas, the starch and bulk of their new outfits prevented it. They sighed.

"Oh, my butt is itching up a storm, and I can't reach it in this monkey suit," groaned Shrek.

He reached back to scratch his behind but had no more luck than he'd had trying to kiss Fiona. It was hopeless!

Then he spied one of the servants carrying a long ruby scepter.

"What's your name?" asked Shrek.

"Eh, Fiddlesworth, sir," replied the man.

"Hoo hoo hooo. Perfect!" chortled Shrek. He asked Fiddlesworth to scratch his butt with the scepter.

At that moment, the curtains began to rise, and the Master of Ceremonies announced: "Ladies and gentlemen, standing in for the king and queen of Far Far Away: Princess Fiona and Sir Shrek!"

The audience cheered. But the applause slowly trailed

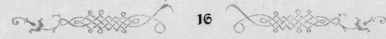

off as, one by one, they noticed Fiddlesworth scratching away at Shrek's butt.

"Scratch it, Fiddler old boy," cried Shrek. "Ahhh! All right, you got it. . . ."

Puss and Donkey exchanged nervous glances.

"Oh, a little over to the left, yeah," said Shrek, still unaware that all eyes were on him and Fiddlesworth.

"Uh, Shrek?" interrupted Fiona.

By now the crowd was gasping in horror.

Fiona struggled desperately to get Shrek's attention.

"Oh, that's it," Shrek continued.

"Shrek!" cried Fiona.

"Oh, get it! Scratch that thing!" sang Shrek.

"SHREK!!"

Startled out of his scratching daze, Shrek finally looked up and saw the eyes of the crowd staring. Fiddlesworth froze. Shrek chuckled nervously. As he did, his belly shook, and his new belt buckle flew off and hit Donkey in the eye.

"Ow! My eye! My eye!" screamed Donkey, stumbling blindly through the ballroom. He grabbed ahold

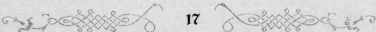

of a lady in the crowd.

"What are you doing?!" she shouted, pushing Donkey away.

Donkey toppled over and fell against a guard who was holding a royal battle-ax. The ax flew out of the guard's hands, sailed past Puss's head, and knocked over a big vase. The vase shot up onstage, and Fiona fielded it. But the slosh of the water in the vase swept her off-balance. She fell and bumped into Shrek, whose collar sprang loose and slapped him in the face, while the clasp holding up his pants let go. Poor Shrek found himself standing onstage with his collar up and his pants down around his ankles.

"Fiona!" he cried in dismay. He shuffled toward her helplessly.

He tripped over his pants and came down on a loose wooden plank in the stage. The other end of the plank rose up like a catapult, sending Fiddlesworth flying through the air.

"Uhhhh . . . ," whimpered Fiddlesworth as he dangled precariously from a high banner pole.

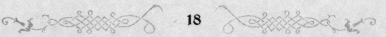

Shrek leaned over Fiona, who was still on the floor. "Are you okay?" he asked.

"Yeah," she sighed. "I'm fine."

Up above they could hear the sound of Fiddlesworth's jacket ripping. The jacket gave way, and the crowd gasped as they watched him plummet—right into a waiter carrying an armload of flaming skewers.

The skewers flew through the air. They whizzed past Donkey and speared the curtains, setting them on fire.

Donkey pulled out one of the skewers, blew out the flame, and took a little bite. "Oh! Shrimp!" he cried. "My favorite!"

As he munched, the fire spread. Soon the ceiling beams were burning. A big shield caught fire and dropped from one of the beams down to the stage floor. The wooden stage came crashing down, sending the buffet tables crashing into Shrek and Fiona.

They stood helplessly amid the chaos, wiping the food and the makeup from their faces, wondering if they would *ever* feel ready to be king and queen.

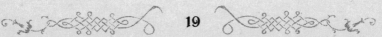

Chapter Three

Shrek stormed into their bedroom that evening. "That's it, Fiona! We're leaving!" he declared.

"Honey, please calm down," crooned Fiona.

"Calm down!? Who do you think we're kidding!?" cried Shrek. "I'm an ogre! I'm not cut out for this, Fiona, and I never will be."

Shrek wiped off his makeup and flung his shirt onto the floor. He fell onto the bed in exasperation.

A head and a pair of hooves popped out from under the covers right beside him. "I think that went pretty well," declared Donkey.

Startled, Shrek's eyes were about to pop out of his head. "Donkey!" he shouted.

He hauled Donkey out of bed and carried him toward the door.

"Oh, c'mon now, Shrek," protested Donkey.

"Out you go!" cried Shrek, giving the pesky equine the boot.

Shrek turned back toward the bed, satisfied, only to see Puss reclining on his pillow!

"Some people just don't understand boundaries," sighed Puss, nodding in Donkey's direction.

Shrek picked the annoying feline up by the scruff of the neck, tossed him out the window, and slammed it shut. Puss peered back in through the glass with his big, sad Puss eyes.

Shrek scowled at him and drew the blinds. Finally alone with Fiona, he lay back in bed.

Fiona tried to soothe him. "Just think, a couple more days and we'll be back home in our vermin-filled shack, strewn with fungus, filled with the rotting stench of mud and neglect. . . ."

 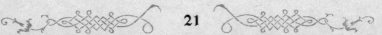

Shrek drew in a deep breath and sighed. For the first time all day he genuinely relaxed. "You had me at 'vermin-filled.'"

"And, uh . . . ," Fiona hesitated, "maybe even the pitter-patter of little feet on the floor . . . ?"

Shrek chuckled. "That's right. The swamp rats will be spawning."

"Uh, no . . . what I was thinking of is a little bit bigger than a swamp rat," said Fiona, uncertain how to tell her husband what was on her mind.

"Donkey?" asked Shrek.

"No, Shrek. Um . . . what if —theoretically—"

"Yeah?" Shrek leaned closer, all ears.

"They were little ogre feet?"

Shrek turned to face her. He stared a moment, speechless.

He took a deep breath. "Oh," he said, tentatively. "Honey? Theoretically, I'm not ready for kids."

"Why not?" asked Fiona.

"Well uh, kids are, I mean . . . ," stammered Shrek. "Have you seen a baby lately? They just eat and poop, and

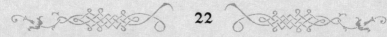

they cry and then they cry when they poop and they poop when they cry and they . . ."

Fiona interrupted him. "Shrek, don't you ever think about having a family?"

Shrek folded her in his great ogre arms and cuddled her close. "Right now, *you* are my family."

He leaned in for the kiss he had waited for all day, when all of a sudden he and Fiona were startled out of their embrace by a loud pounding on the door.

As they looked up, the door burst open. The royal page stood at attention in the doorway and cried, "Princess Fiona!"

Shrek groaned. Interrupted again! "Well," he huffed, "somebody had better be dying."

Chapter Four

The page hurried Shrek and Fiona to the king's bedroom, where they found him lying on his lily pad, coughing.

"I'm dying," he told them. He took in a deep breath and launched into a violent coughing fit.

Shrek gave Fiona a guilty look.

Queen Lillian stood by her husband's bedside. "Harold," she said soothingly.

"Don't forget to pay the gardener, Lillian," he replied.

"Of course, darling," she said, humoring him. She had grown accustomed to his random thoughts since the

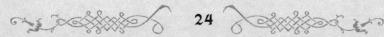

Fairy Godmother had turned him back into a frog.

"Fiona . . . ," sputtered the king, holding back another coughing fit.

"Yes, Daddy?"

"I know I've made many mistakes with you."

"It's okay," whispered Fiona.

"But your love for Shrek has taught me so much."

Fiona smiled.

He turned toward Shrek. "My dear boy, I am proud to call you my son."

Shrek smiled, too.

"Now, there is a matter of business to attend toooo. . . ."

They looked on helplessly as the king was seized by another coughing fit.

Fiona and Shrek leaned over him. His breathing stopped!

Puss swept the plumed hat off his head with a flourish. "The Frog King is dead," he declared.

Fiona's eyes filled up with tears.

Suddenly the king gasped for another breath and began coughing again.

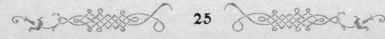

Donkey nudged Puss. "Put your hat back on, fool," he whispered.

"Shrek, please come hither," commanded the king.

Fiona gave Shrek a worried look.

"Yeah, Dad?" Shrek asked, moving closer.

"This kingdom needs a new king. You and Fiona are next in line for the throne."

"Oooo. Next in line," repeated Shrek nervously. "Now you see, Dad, that's why people love you. Even on your deathbed you're still making jokes."

The king stared back at him, stone-faced.

"Oh, come on, there's got to be somebody else," dithered Shrek. "Anybody?"

"Aside from you there is only one remaining heir," replied the king.

Shrek brightened with hope. "Really!? Who is he?"

"His name is . . ." The king gasped for breath. "Is . . ."

Shrek and Fiona leaned closer, desperate to hear the name. The king stopped breathing and fell back on his lily pad.

"Daddy!" wailed Fiona.

A fly escaped from the king's mouth.

Puss's plumed hat came off once more.

Suddenly the king's froggy tongue darted out and caught the fly again.

Puss quickly put his hat back on.

"His name is Arthur," said the king, chewing the fly.

"Arthur?" asked Shrek.

"I know . . . you'll do . . . what's riiiiiiiiiiight . . . ," wheezed the king with his last breath.

Fiona burst into tears and threw her arms around her husband. Shrek could only stand there like a statue— speechless and in shock.

Donkey bowed his head. "Do your thing, man," he said, nudging Puss.

Puss took off his hat and this time held it to his heart. Queen Lillian, Shrek, and Fiona bowed their heads and stood at the Frog King's bedside, letting the reality of his death sink in.

The devoted citizens of Far Far Away quietly closed up their shops and prepared for the royal funeral. Their beloved Frog King was laid out in a little shoebox. As a

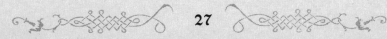

frog choir sang a farewell song to their king, Queen Lillian gently set the box atop a lily pad and let it float out into the pond. Shrek and Fiona and all the fairy-tale creatures looked on.

But unseen by all, peering down from the distant hillside, was a mysterious cloaked figure on horseback. He smiled smugly at what he saw. The Land of Far Far Away was at its weakest. Now was the time to take action!

Chapter
Five

The cloaked figure was, of course, none other than the dastardly Prince Charming. After the funeral, he rode to The Poison Apple Inn, strutted through the doors, and surveyed the scene. Rumplestiltskin chatted with a friend, while Captain Hook played tunes at the piano and a vile witch sang along. The evil Puppet Master was drowning his sorrows in beer, while the big Cyclops rode the medieval mechanical bull. In the corner, Snow White's Evil Queen was playing a game of pool with another one of the witches.

Without taking his eyes off the crowd of villains,

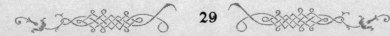

Prince Charming removed his cloak and hung it on the branch of an evil tree. The tree considered the cloak for a moment and then flung it on the grimy stone floor. Although the fairy-tale villains never stopped what they were doing, all eyes turned to Prince Charming and followed his every move. What was the precious golden-haired prince doing in a place like this?

He pulled a white handkerchief from his pocket, laid it over a bar stool daintily, and sat down.

He cleared his throat dramatically, hoping to get his old friend Doris's attention. "What does a prince have to do to get a drink around here?"

But it was Mabel, Cinderella's other ugly stepsister, who rose up from behind the bar.

"Where's Doris?" asked Charming. "Taking the night off?"

"She's not welcome here," growled Mabel in her manly voice, "and neither are you!" She spat into an empty beer mug and wiped it with her towel. "What do you want, Charming?"

"Oh, not much. Just a chance at redemption." He

laughed. "And a Fuzzy Navel."

Charming rose from his stool and addressed the crowd: "And Fuzzy Navels for all my friends!"

The villains stopped what they were doing and eyed him suspiciously. Captain Hook raked his hook across the piano keys.

"We're not your friends," he growled.

Prince Charming twittered nervously.

Suddenly Mabel grabbed him by the shoulders and pinned him to the bar.

"Ahhh," he gasped.

The captain placed his hook against Charming's throat. "You don't belong here," he threatened.

"You're right, you're absolutely right," stammered Prince Charming, "but do any of us?"

"Do a number on his face!" cried the Cyclops.

"No, no, wait, wait, wait!" cried Charming, thinking fast. "We are more alike than you think."

"Cry me a river, pretty boy!" sneered the Evil Queen.

Charming saw an opportunity to get the villains over to his side. He turned toward the queen. "The Seven

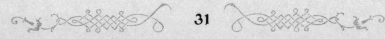

Dwarfs saved Snow White, and then what happened?" asked Charming.

"Oh, what's it to you?" asked the queen.

"They left you the un-fairest of them all. And now here you are, hustling pool to get your next meal. How does that feel?" he asked, pouring on the charm.

"Pretty unfair," replied the queen.

"And you!" cried Charming, turning to address the Puppet Master. "Your star puppet abandons the show to go and find his father."

"I hate that little wooden puppet," whined the Puppet Master.

"And Hook . . ." Prince Charming paused dramatically and looked down at the steel hook against his throat. "Need I say more?"

Hook backed off, feeling insecure about his metal appendage.

"And you, Frumpypigskin."

"Rumplestiltskin," he corrected Charming crossly.

"Where's that firstborn you were promised, eh?"

As the villains responded, Prince Charming's confi-

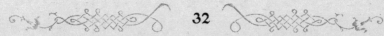

dence grew. He looked Mabel in the eye. "Remember how you couldn't get your little fat foot into that tiny glass slipper?"

Mabel nodded.

"Well, Cinderella is in Far Far Away right now, eating bonbons and cavorting with every last little fairy-tale creature that has ever done you wrong.

"Once upon a time, someone decided that we were the losers. But there are two sides to every story. And our side has not been told!"

By now, all the villains were listening to Prince Charming with rapt attention.

"So who will join me?" he asked. "Who wants to come out on top for once? Who wants their happily-ever-after?"

The crowd of villains shouted and cheered and started getting rowdy. Before he knew it, Prince Charming was standing in the middle of a barroom brawl. He ducked as a bottle flew past his head. He kept his head down and sipped his Fuzzy Navel, trying to figure out how he was going to organize this pack of villains, now that he had their attention.

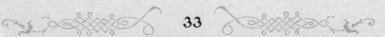

Chapter Six

Down at the docks, it was time for Shrek, Donkey, and Puss to bid their loved ones a tearful farewell, as they set out in search of the fabled Arthur.

Puss took his latest love in his arms. "It is out of my hands, señorita, the winds of fate have blown on my destiny. But I will never forget you. You are the love of my life."

At that, another love of Puss's life approached. He glanced over at her with moony eyes. "As are you . . ."

Before long, several other pretty kitties arrived.

"And you. And you," Puss continued enthusiastically. "And, uh . . ." He spotted another he hadn't even met. "I don't know you, but I'd like to. I gotta go!"

As he made his escape, he could hear the sound of cats fighting behind him. He darted past Dragon, who was trying to hold back her tears as she said good-bye to her Donkey dearest.

She let out a soft, dragony wail.

"I know, I know," crooned Donkey. "I don't want to leave you either, baby, but you know how Shrek is. The dude's lost without me."

She smiled a tender, understanding smile.

"But don't worry, I'll send you airmail kisses every day," promised Donkey.

Holding back tears of his own, he looked down at his brood of little Dronkeys. "All right, be strong, babies! Be strong!" he cajoled. "Now Coco, Peanut, you listen to Mama, all right? And Bananas, no more roastin' marshmallows on your sister's head."

"Kerchooooo!" Bananas let out a fiery sneeze.

"Ah," cried Donkey, "that's my special boy. Oh, come

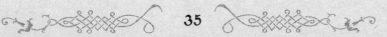

over here, all of you. Give your Daddy a big hug."

Fiona was cuddling one of the Dronkeys. She sent him off to join his siblings and watched fondly as all the little ones swooped and swarmed around their dad.

"Well, this is it," said Shrek, walking up to her.

Fiona took a deep breath to brace herself. "Shrek, there's something I have to tell you."

"I know," said Shrek. "Your mother was hoping we'd stay. But c'mon, Fiona, you and I both know that anybody would be a better king than me."

"It's not that. No, it's just . . . you see . . . ," Fiona stammered. "I really wish you weren't leaving right now because . . ."

"I know. Me, too," interrupted Shrek. "But don't worry, we'll be back with this Arthur guy before you know it."

Fiona didn't look convinced.

"And if he gives me any trouble, I've always got persuasion and reason," he said, as he held up his right and left fists. "You'll see," he tried to soothe her. "Soon it's finally going to be just you and me."

"It's not going to be just you and me. . . ."

The ship's horn sounded, and the captain shouted, "ALL ABOARD!"

"Ah, c'mon. It will be. I promise," said Shrek distractedly. "I promise. I love you."

Fiona struggled to get the words out, but everything was happening so fast. Shrek gave her a big kiss. And before she knew it, he was aboard the boat, standing beside Donkey and Puss. The three friends waved from the gunwales. Up in the sky, the little Dronkeys spelled out "We Love You, Daddy" in streams of smoke.

"*Awwwwwwwww,*" cried all the fairy-tale creatures who had gathered to bid Shrek and his friends farewell.

Donkey wiped the tears from his eyes. "Bye-bye, babies!"

Shrek waved to Fiona.

"Shrek!" she cried, running after the boat as it began to pull away. She had to tell him!

"What?" asked Shrek.

"Wait!" she cried in desperation.

"What is it?" shouted Shrek.

She smiled, took a deep breath, and called out, "I'm . . . I'm . . ."

The captain blew the whistle again, and it drowned out her voice.

Shrek smiled back, not hearing a word. "I love you, too, honey!"

"No . . . No, I said I'm pr—"

The horn sounded once again.

Shrek grabbed the horn and tossed it overboard. "You're what?"

"I said, I'm pregnant!" Fiona shouted.

The fairy-tale creatures began to cheer.

Shrek rubbed an ear in disbelief. "You're what!?"

"You're going to be a father!" cried Fiona.

Shrek stood there for a moment, speechless. He laughed nervously. "That's great," he said.

"I know!" cried Fiona. "I love you!"

Shrek smiled weakly. "Yeah . . . heh, heh. . . . Me, too . . . you. . . ."

Queen Lillian put her arm around Fiona, and they

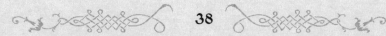

stood on the dock waving until the boat disappeared into the mist.

Overjoyed at the news, Donkey leapt up on the gunwales and cheered. "I'm gonna be an uncle! I'm gonna be an uncle!"

Puss just shook his head knowingly at Shrek. "And you, my friend, are in royal trouble."

Chapter Seven

As the boat rocked on the waves that night, Shrek fell fast asleep in his bunk. Before he knew it, he was in dreamland, and the boat was chugging up a wide river. It looked so familiar!

"Ahhh, home," he sighed, as the boat went aground on soft sand. He smiled to himself and wiped a tear of happiness from his eye.

He leapt off the boat and took in the scene. Right there in front of him was his beloved swamp house. "Woo-hoo!" he shouted. He took in a deep breath of the fetid air and sighed blissfully.

"Shrek!?" He heard Fiona calling him. He skipped

 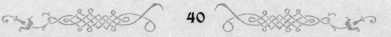

toward home, dancing and giggling like a delighted child.

He sashayed through the door, closing his eyes and opening his arms for a big hug.

But there was no hug. "Fiona?" he called. The room was silent. He looked all around, puzzled. Suddenly he heard the door click shut behind him. He turned to see a mysterious baby carriage covered with a blanket. He lifted the corner of the blanket and peered in. A little baby ogre smiled up at him sweetly!

"Huh? Oh, no," moaned Shrek.

The baby burped.

Shrek smiled. "Better out than in, I always say."

Hiccup! Suddenly the baby was vomiting all over Shrek. He put up his hands to shield himself from the deluge. But it was no use! Soon, both he and the baby were completely covered in it. The baby looked like he was going to cry.

"Ha, ha. No, no, no, no, no, no. It's gonna be all right," twittered Shrek. He took the baby awkwardly in his arms and tried to manage a sweet, fatherly smile.

"Da-da!" cried the baby.

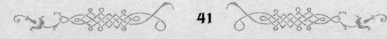

Suddenly the whole swamp house was filled with babies! They tumbled around the living room, tearing fabric off the chairs, knocking glass jars off the shelves, and pulling the dishes and cutlery off the table. The knives stuck in the floorboards, and babies wove in and out between them.

"Hey!" cried Shrek in a panic. "Hey, hey wait! No, no. Stop! Hey, hey, hey. . . ."

One of the babies struck a match. Shrek scooped him up in his arms and blew out the flame. Another baby had to be rescued from the big iron cauldron in the fireplace. One by one, Shrek picked the babies up and placed them in the carriage.

Suddenly he heard a loud rumble, and babies began pouring out of the fireplace. There were dozens of them! They were breaking the glass and tumbling in through the windows, too.

Shrek abandoned the carriage and ran for the door. But no matter how fast he ran, the door kept getting farther and farther away.

Finally, breathless and exhausted, he reached it. Hundreds of babies gurgled and burped and toddled toward him. He dashed through the door and slammed it shut behind him. He leaned his back against the door, closed his eyes, and sighed in relief. But when he opened his eyes again, he found himself onstage at his old high school. The banner in the back of the auditorium read: CONGRATULATIONS GRADS—CLASS OF 976 A.D. Thousands of ogre babies sat in the audience. They were laughing and pointing at him. Shrek looked at himself, only to realize that he was standing onstage stark naked!

"Ahhhhhhh!!!" Shrek was shouting when the ship's horn sounded. His eyes popped open and he sat upright in his bunk. "Donkey! Donkey, wake up!"

Donkey and Puss seemed to turn slowly toward him. But both of them had baby ogre faces!

Donkey's eyes glowed red, and when he smiled, he showed little pointy teeth. "Da-da!" he cried.

"Ahhhhhhhhhhhhhhhhhhhh!" Shrek screamed.

Donkey and Puss woke up and stared at him, alarmed.

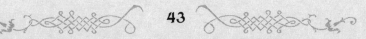

"Shrek! Shrek, are you okay?" cried Donkey.

"Oh...," moaned Shrek. "I can't believe I'm going to be a father."

Donkey and Puss exchanged worried glances.

Shrek leaned over the ship's railing and tried to compose himself. "How did this happen?" he whined.

"Allow me to explain," offered Puss. "You see, when a man has certain feelings for a woman, a powerful urge sweeps over him, and ..."

"I know *how* it happened!" growled Shrek. "I just can't believe it."

Shrek leaned over the rail again and stared hopelessly at the water.

Puss hopped up on the railing next to him and whispered in his ear. "You know I love Fiona, boss. Right? But what I'm talking about here is you, me, my cousin's boat, an ice-cold pitcher of mojitos, and two weeks of nothing but fishing."

Donkey cozied up to Shrek and whispered in his other ear. "Man, don't you listen to him. Look, you're

gonna love having kids. It's like living your childhood all over again."

Shrek stared at him for a moment in horror.

"Okay, okay I get it, so you didn't have a happy childhood," said Donkey. "That doesn't mean having a baby is gonna ruin your life."

"Well, it's not my life I'm worried about. It's the kid's." Shrek's ears drooped, and he hung his head.

"I'm doomed," he sighed.

"You'll be fine," said Donkey.

"You're finished," said the ship's captain.

Donkey, Shrek, and Puss looked at him.

The captain cleared his throat. "Uh, with your journey."

He pointed to the shore. There on a high bluff stood a majestic castle.

"Whoa," cried Donkey. "Arthur must be some kind of big shot. I mean, look at that castle!"

Puss leapt on Shrek's shoulder. "We'll find Fiona's cousin, and your problems will be over, *jefe*! Well, except for the baby thing."

Chapter Eight

Shrek, Donkey, and Puss stood across the moat from the castle, and Donkey squinted to read the sign over the gate. "Wor-ces-ter-shireee," he sounded out.

"It's Worcestershire," said Shrek.

"Oh, like the sauce. Mmmmm . . ." Donkey smacked his lips.

They watched as the drawbridge slowly creaked down.

"Oooo, they must be expecting us!" cried Donkey.

They'd begun to march across when they heard a horse whinnying behind them. They turned to see it galloping

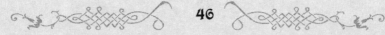

toward them, pulling a busload of schoolchildren. The three friends jumped out of the way to let the vehicle go by.

The children screamed in horror at the sight of Shrek.

Donkey was puzzled. "What in the shista-shire kind of place is this?"

Shrek shuddered. "My stomach aches and my palms just got sweaty. Must be a high school."

"High school!?" cried Donkey.

Inside the courtyard, they caught sight of a group of medieval cheerleaders practicing their cheers.

"Ready?" shouted the leader. "Okay! Whither art thou headed—to the top?"

"Yea, we think so! We think so!" the group responded.

"And dost thou thinkest we can be stopped!?"

"Nay, we thinks not! We thinks not!"

Shrek rolled his eyes and stalked past.

"Ahhhhhhhhhh!" A startled kid ran off toward the parking lot, where carriages of all different shapes and sizes were parked.

A horse and carriage crossed in front of Shrek, and he

read the sign on the back: CAUTION—STUDENT DRIVER.

Shrek, Puss, and Donkey could hear the instructor anxiously advising a new driver. "All right, Mr. Percival, just ease up on the reins." The three friends cringed as the horse suddenly jumped, sending the carriage jolting sideways into a tree.

Shrek, Donkey, and Puss looked on while, in their imaginations, they relived their own high school days.

"I'm already starting to feel nauseous from memories of wedgies and swirlies," moaned Donkey.

Puss eyed him curiously. "But how did you receive the wedgies when you are clearly not the wearer of the underpants?"

"Let's just say some things are better left unsaid and leave it at that, *por favor*," said Donkey.

They paused to listen to two girls who were huddled together under a medieval arch, discussing their love lives.

"So then I was all like, 'I'd rather get the black plague and lock myself in an iron maiden than go out with you,'" said one.

"Eh, totally," agreed the other.

"Uh, pardon me," said Shrek, approaching them.

"Eh! Totally ew-eth," cried one.

"Yeah, totally!" agreed the other, as they fled in terror.

In another corner of the courtyard, a couple of dorky guys were playing *Dungeons & Dragons*.

"Yes!" they heard one shout. "I've just altered my character level to plus-three superability!"

Shrek went up to them. "Hi, we're looking for someone named . . ."

"Gee," the boy interrupted him. "Who rolled a plus-nine 'dork' spell and summoned the beast and his quadrupeds?"

The other boy guffawed and snorted violently in delight. Suddenly his nose began to bleed, and he panicked as if he'd been mortally injured.

Shrek rolled his eyes. "Can either of you teenage maladroits tell me where I can find Arthur?" he asked.

The boy leaned his head back and desperately tried to stop the nosebleed.

"He's over there," said the first boy, pointing toward the athletic field.

Shrek could see a bold knight in shining armor astride his white steed. The horse reared up, eager and ready to charge. The three friends hurried to the field just in time for the joust. The knight's horse pawed the sand. His nostrils flared. The knight kept his eyes steady on his opponent—and then charged!

The other knight's eyes widened in fear as the bold knight approached. WHAM! The lance hit, sending him flying through the air over Shrek's head.

Shrek looked at the triumphant knight, who removed his helmet to show off his handsome face and satisfied grin.

"There is no sweeter taste on thy tongue than victory!" cried the knight.

"Oy! Right! Ooo! Ooo! Ooo!" cheered the other jocks in the audience.

Shrek was impressed. He turned to Puss. "Does Arthur look like a king or what!?"

He smiled and stepped toward the victorious knight.

"Ow," came a small voice from below.

Shrek looked down and saw that he had stepped square on the chest of the knight's opponent. "Oh, sorry," he said.

The losing knight didn't budge. He just lay there with his legs and arms still sprawled out, exactly where he had hit the ground. "Did you just say you were looking for Arthur?" he asked.

"That information is on a need-to-know basis," replied Puss.

"Is he in trouble?" asked Artie.

"It's top secret, hushity-hush," added Donkey.

"Yeah sure, no problem," said the kid. "But just to let you know—he prefers to go by his nickname, Peaches."

Shrek looked skeptical.

"Peaches?" asked Donkey.

"Peaches," declared the teenager.

Shrek wiggled his ears, perplexed.

"Now, let's away to the showers!" the victorious knight was shouting.

"Oy! Right! Ooo! Ooo! Ooo!" shouted the jocks in unison.

But at the sight of the big ogre, the knight's horse reared up in fear, and the knight came crashing to the ground.

Shrek stood over him. "Greetings, Your Majesty. This is your lucky day. Your kingdom awaits."

"So what, like, are you supposed to be?" asked the knight. "Some kind of giant mutant leprechaun or something?"

"Yeah, right, sure," replied Shrek. "I'm a giant mutant leprechaun." At that he scooped up the knight, tossed him over his shoulder, and carried him off.

"Unhand me, monster!" shouted the knight.

"Calm down, Peaches," teased Shrek.

"What did you call me?" cried the knight.

"Peaches," said Donkey.

"Peaches," added Puss.

"Stop calling me that!" the knight shouted indignantly.

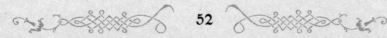

Shrek lugged the reluctant knight toward the gate.

"Fine," said Shrek, "but we're late for your coronation, Arthur."

"I am not Arthur!" declared the knight.

Shrek stopped short, held him out at arm's length, and studied him, eye to eye.

"I am Lancelot," said the knight proudly.

Shrek looked back over his shoulder and saw Lancelot's defeated opponent racing away.

"Hey!" Shrek shouted.

Arthur glanced back at Shrek, then turned and kept on going.

Shrek dropped Lancelot to the ground and stormed off after Arthur. Donkey and Puss trotted behind Shrek, trying to catch up.

One of the cheerleaders waved to get Shrek's attention. "Ahem! This is, like, totally embarrassing, but my friend, Tiffany, thinkest thou vex her so soothly . . ."

Shrek stopped to listen, but he had no idea what she was trying to say.

". . . and she thought perchance thou would wanna

ask her to the Homecoming Dance or something. . . ."

"Uh, excuse me?" cried Shrek.

"It's like, whatever," the cheerleader continued. "She's just totally into college guys and mythical creatures and stuff."

While she popped her gum, Shrek, Puss, and Donkey darted into the school to search the classrooms for the elusive Arthur.

Chapter Nine

Oh, Ar-thur! Come out, come out, wherever you are . . . ," called Shrek. The students were too frightened of Shrek to pester him, but poor Donkey soon found himself being stuffed into a locker. A group of teenagers giggled and pointed at him as he struggled to free himself from the tight quarters.

He treated them to a ferocious glare. "You'd better run, you little punk no-goodniks, 'cause the days of 'Little Donkey Dumpy Drawers' are over!"

But the scoundrels had already taped an I STINK-ETH sign to the back of his neck.

They ran off, giggling harder than ever.

Suddenly Puss called out: "Check it out, Boss! Arturo at two o'clock!"

They saw Arthur darting into the gymnasium, where the entire student body had gathered for a pep rally.

Principal Pynchley stood in the center of the gym holding a megaphone up to his mouth. Students filled the bleachers on each side. Pynchley was just thanking Professor Primbottom for his invigorating lecture on how to "Just Say Nay," when two students stepped up on either side of him, one dressed up as a dragon, the other as a griffin.

Pynchley greeted the two students. "And now, without further ado," he cried through the megaphone, "let's give a warm Worcestershire-huzzah to the winner of our New Mascot Contest . . ."

Suddenly the doors of the gymnasium burst open, and everyone turned to see Shrek's enormous, terrifying bulk framed in the doorway.

". . . the ogre!?" said Pynchley.

The band started to play, and the students began to cheer.

The student dressed as a griffin pulled off his mask and threw it to the ground. "It was supposed to be me!" he fumed. He kicked the mask and stormed away, sulking.

Shrek scanned the bleachers in search of Artie.

"This is all indeed a bit unorthodox," dithered Pynchley, about to declare the ogre the new school mascot.

Shrek grabbed the megaphone from the principal's hand. "Thanks so much, let's win the big game against the visitors."

The crowd sat in silence.

"Come on out, Arthur! I know you're in here!" Shrek yelled.

The crowd suddenly burst into a fit of laughter. Shrek, Puss, and Donkey slowly turned around to find Artie attached to the nearby basketball hoop, suspended by his underwear.

"Hi, there! Remember me? Do you mind coming down, 'cause we need to get going. You're the new king of Far Far Away."

The crowd gasped in surprise. Then, one by one, the students began to giggle.

"Artie a king? More like the Mayor of Loserville!" taunted Lancelot.

By now the whole audience was roaring with laughter.

It was humiliating! All Artie could do was hang in the air in silent fury.

"Hey, that's royalty you're messing with," Shrek growled.

"I didn't do it. They did," Lancelot said defensively. He pointed to a group of nerds who were standing in the corner doubled over in laughter. One of the boys snorted so hard that his nose began to bleed.

Puss leapt through the air and cut Artie free from the basketball hoop. He fell right into Shrek's arms.

"Is this for real?" asked Artie.

"Yep, let's go get you fitted for your crown," Shrek said.

As they headed toward the exit, the school band played "Hail to the Chief."

Artie's face lit up with excitement.

"Give me just a second," said Artie.

Artie turned to face the crowd and cleared his throat.

"Well, well, well. Look who's a king. Farewell, Lance. Hey, if there's any justice in the world, next time I run into you, you'll be manager of Friar's Fat Boy!"

Lancelot glowered.

"And you guys here," Artie said, addressing the nerds who had hung him up by his underwear, "you can expect a little visit from my knights!"

"And Gwen, I've always loved you."

At the sound of this statement, Guinevere and her friend looked at each other in shock.

"Well, good friends, it breaks my heart, but I've got to go. Enjoy your stay in prison while I rule the free world!"

"All right, let's not overdo it," said Shrek.

"I'm building my city, people!" replied an excited Artie.

Shrek grabbed him by the arm and led him out of the gymnasium.

Chapter Ten

While Shrek was off in search of Arthur, Queen Lillian and the princesses in Far Far Away planned a baby shower for Fiona. When the day came, they gathered in the castle library. The princesses gasped in admiration as Fiona arrived in her fancy new maternity gown. Two sweet birdies picked up a crown of flowers in their beaks and placed it on the new mother's head.

"Look at you!" cried Snow White.

"Wow!" cheered Rapunzel.

"You look darling!" gushed Snow White.

 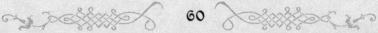

Sleeping Beauty woke up for the occasion. "You must be due any day now, you're absolutely huge!"

"Ooooh! It's present time!" sang Snow White, breaking the awkward silence. The birds and little forest creatures flocked around her, twittering and chirping.

Cinderella pointed excitedly at the big pile of gifts. "Oh, Fiona, won't you please open mine first!? It's the one in front!"

Fiona read the card: "Congratulations on your new mess maker. Hopefully this will help." She paused and chuckled uncomfortably at the joke.

She unwrapped the package and pulled out a plastic bag and pooper-scooper.

The princesses ooooo'd and ahhhhhh'd over the gift.

"Will you look at that," said Doris.

Sleeping Beauty opened her eyes and asked, "What is it?"

"I'm glad you like it. It's for the poopies," chirped Cinderella.

"Fiona! Fiona!" cried the other fairy-tale creatures, trying to get her attention.

"We all chipped in for a present, too," cried one of the Little Pigs.

Pinocchio spun around and presented Fiona with a fancy baby carrier.

"Ta-dah!" cried the Gingerbread Man, popping out from inside.

"Oooooooo," crooned the princesses.

"You know the baby's gonna love it, because I do!" cried Gingy.

"Oh, you guys, that's so sweet," said Fiona. "Thank you."

She began to open the next present. "Who's this one from?" she asked.

"I got you the biggest one because I love you the most," cried Snow White.

The other princesses scowled at her.

Fiona opened up the box. Inside stood a dwarf in a little green hat.

Fiona couldn't believe her eyes. "Um . . . what is it?" she asked.

"He's a live-in babysitter," explained Snow White.

The dwarf stretched out his arms. "Where's the baby?"

"You're too kind, Snow," said Fiona, "but I can't accept this."

"Think nothing of it," said Snow White. "I've got six more at home!"

"What does he do?" asked Fiona tentatively.

"The cleaning!" declared Cinderella.

"The feeding!" cried Snow White.

"The burping," added the dwarf.

"So, what are Shrek and I supposed to do?" asked Fiona.

"Well," said Rapunzel, "now you'll have plenty of time to work on your marriage."

Fiona put her hands on her hips. "What's that supposed to mean?"

"Oh, come on now, Fiona," crooned Rapunzel. "You know what happens."

"Huh?" asked Sleeping Beauty, coming out of her doze. "You're tired all the time . . . ?"

"You'll start letting yourself go," declared Snow White.

"Stretch marks!" squeaked Gingy.

"Oh, and don't expect Shrek to be too helpful," said

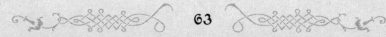

Rapunzel. "He'll be out with his buddies all night. Say good-bye to romance."

Dragon poked her head through the window. "YORT!" she cried.

"Um, how many of you have kids?" demanded Fiona.

Besides Dragon, not one of them did! They hemmed and hawed and shrugged.

"She's right," said Doris. "A baby is only gonna strengthen the love that Shrek and Fiona have. How did Shrek react when you told him, Fiona? Tell me!"

"Oh, Shrek? Oh, well, he was, uh, very . . . he was really . . . ," Fiona stammered. She laughed nervously, trying to hide the worried expression on her face, while outside the window she heard odd noises. Even more worrisome—she thought she heard Dragon let out a fearful, rumbling roar.

Chapter Eleven

Alas, as the princesses and fairy-tale creatures partied in the castle, the sky above Far Far Away was darkening with villains from The Poison Apple. They rode on broomsticks, and Prince Charming led the way.

"Onward, my new friends!" he cried. "To our happily-ever-after!" He threw back his head and laughed an evil laugh. Suddenly a bug flew into his mouth. *"Gaa! Ahhhh!"* He picked the bug out and tossed it in disgust.

"Now, bombs away!" he cried.

Evil trees were hanging under some of the broomsticks

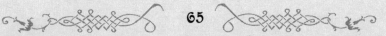

like bombs. The broomstick pilots moved into "V" formation. They swooped down and released their payload.

The evil trees pulled their branches, and their leafy parachutes opened up with a whoosh. They landed amid the shoppers on the streets below. People everywhere screamed and fled in terror!

An evil knight scared away the customers at the coffee shop and proceeded to drink all the unfinished cups of coffee.

Captain Hook tried to snatch a little boy away from his mother.

"Well, well, well. If it isn't Peter Pan," he cried.

"His name's not Peter!" shouted the terrified mother.

"Shut it, Wendy!" growled Hook.

Another villain threw a cart through a store window. The big Cyclops gleefully pulled letters out of the mailbox, ripped the stamps off, and stuffed them back in.

Prince Charming swooped downtown on his broomstick and tried to get them back on task.

"To the castle!" he ordered his troops.

The evil witches and other villains fell in line behind

him. Soon they had the castle surrounded.

"Roarrrrrr!!!" Dragon roasted one of them with her fiery breath. But more villains zoomed in to circle her.

Hearing Dragon's roar again, Fiona leaned out the window to find out what was happening. She spotted a group of witches dropping a heavy metal net over Dragon.

"Roarrrrrr!!!" Dragon cried.

"It's a siege!" squeaked the Gingerbread Man, slamming the library door shut.

The Three Pigs and Pinocchio pushed a dresser and a few chairs in front of it. The little fairy-tale creatures braced themselves against the furniture, hoping to hold the villains out.

"Fiona, you go and take care of the baby!" piped Gingy bravely.

The princesses panicked.

"Everybody stay calm," cried Snow White. "We're all going to die!"

Fiona took charge. She pushed on the side of the fireplace, and a secret door opened up, revealing an underground passageway. "Everyone in! Now!" she ordered.

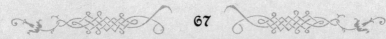 

Outside the library door, Prince Charming and the villains were using one of the evil trees as a battering ram.

"C'mon. Put some back into it, people!" cried Charming.

Cyclops sat astride the tree like a mechanical bull, whooping gleefully. "Yee-haw!"

Boom! Boom! Boom!

The door was beginning to give way!

"We don't have much time. Now go!" cried Fiona, ordering the princesses down the stairs.

"We'll hold them off as long as we can!" squeaked little Gingy.

One more loud *boom*, and the door burst open. Prince Charming and the villains stalked into the room.

The fairy-tale creatures had quickly arranged themselves around the table, pretending to have an innocent little tea party.

"Where are Shrek and Fiona?" demanded Prince Charming.

"Names don't ring a bell," said Gingy nonchalantly.

"Yah," agreed one of the Pigs.

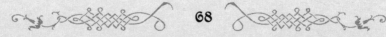

"No bell," added another.

They sipped their tea with measured calm.

"I suggest you freaks cooperate with the new king of Far Far Away," threatened Prince Charming.

"The only thing you're ever gonna be king of is 'King of the Stupids,'" blurted Gingy.

Charming snapped his fingers. "Hook!"

"Avast ye cookie!" cried Captain Hook, raising his hook under Gingy's chin. "Start talkin'!"

Poor Gingy tried to be strong, but he was soon out like a light. As his whole life passed before his white-icing eyes, he sang: *"On the good ship Lollypop, it's a sweet trip to the candy shop . . ."*

Prince Charming gritted his teeth in frustration. He grabbed Pinocchio's head in his hands and shouted, "You! You can't lie. So tell me, puppet. Where is Shrek!?"

Pinocchio thought for a moment. "Well, I don't know where he's not," he said tentatively.

Charming scowled and eyed the little puppet. "You're telling me you don't know where Shrek is?"

Pinocchio fidgeted. "Well . . . it wouldn't be inaccurate to assume that I couldn't exactly not say that that is or isn't almost partially incorrect," he tried.

"So, you do know where he is!" cried Charming.

"On the contrary," said Pinocchio, gaining confidence, "I'm possibly, more or less, not definitely rejecting the idea that in no way, with any amount of uncertainty, that . . ."

"Stop it!" shouted Charming.

". . . I undeniably do or do not know where he shouldn't probably be," concluded Pinocchio.

Captain Hook rubbed his aching head. Even the Three Pigs were getting frustrated.

"If that indeed wasn't where he isn't," added Pinocchio, for good measure. "Even if he wasn't not where I knew he was, it could mean that I wouldn't completely not know where he wasn't."

On top of Pinocchio's babble, Gingy kept singing his loopy song. ". . . Lemonade stands, everywhere . . ."

"Oh, enough!" shouted the first Little Pig. The torture

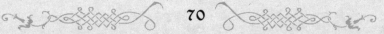

was too much for him! "Shrek went off to bring back the next heir," he confessed.

When he realized his mistake, he gasped and put his cloven hoof over his mouth in horror.

Pinocchio tittered.

"He's bringing back the next heir?" demanded Charming.

"No!" shouted Pinocchio. His nose began to grow.

Prince Charming grinned in satisfaction. He turned to his villainous pals. "Hook, take care of this new king. But bring Shrek to me!" he ordered.

"He'll never fall for your tricks!" cried Pinocchio, his nose growing and growing.

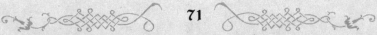

Chapter Twelve

Shrek, Donkey, and Puss finally set sail from Worcestershire, with an extremely excited young Artie. The high school, with its towers and turrets, was just a shrinking dot on the horizon as the boat plowed through the open sea.

"This is going to be great! Thanks for getting me out of there, Shrek. That place was a dead end. But this? Whoo! I can't wait for the parties, princesses, and castles. Look, I know it's not all fun and games. I'm sure I'll have to knight a few heroes, launch a ship or two?"

"Just make sure you hit the boat just right with

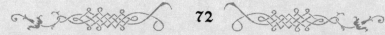

bottle," joked Shrek.

"But seriously . . . me a king? I knew I came from royalty and all, but I just figured everyone forgot about me."

Artie looked out at the sea pensively. "Am I really the only heir?" he asked.

Shrek hesitated a second. "The one and only," he lied.

Artie let out a deep sigh and stared out at sea.

"It's true, Artie," said Donkey. "You'll be living in the lap of luxury. They've got the finest chefs around, waiting for you to place your order."

"And fortunately you'll have the royal food tasters," added Puss.

"What do they do?" asked Artie.

Puss leapt up onto the railing next to him. "They taste the food before the king eats, to make sure it's not poisoned."

"Poisoned!" cried Artie.

"Or too salty," Shrek chimed in, trying to do some damage control.

"Don't worry about it," said Donkey. "You'll be safe and sound with the help of your bodyguards!"

"What!?" cried Artie.

 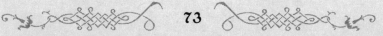

"All of them willing at a moment's notice to lay down his own life out of devotion to you," said Puss with great passion.

Artie looked as if he was about to faint. "Really?" he peeped.

"Indeed!" cried Puss. "You will bask in the affection of your subjects."

"Just make sure your subjects don't die of famine," advised Donkey.

"Or plague," added Puss.

"Ooooh, plague is bad," agreed Donkey.

"And the coughing, the groaning, the festering sores . . . ," Puss shuddered, unable to stop himself.

Shrek forced a laugh again. "Oh! Festering sores!" he chided. "Hey, you are one funny kitty cat."

"What did I say?" Puss asked innocently.

"We don't want Artie here getting the wrong idea," said Shrek. He gestured toward the young king. But the king had vanished!

"Uh, Artie!?" called Shrek.

Suddenly the boat pitched hard to the right. Donkey

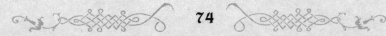

and Puss tumbled across the deck, and Shrek grabbed for the railing.

"Whoa!" they all cried.

The captain slid across the deck in front of them. "Whoa!" he cried.

Artie was at the wheel. He spun it around violently, turning the ship back toward his school in Worcestershire.

"Artie!" shouted Shrek. He dashed toward him. "What are you doing!?"

Shrek grabbed the wheel and tried to steer the boat back on course.

Artie fell to the deck and slid. He spotted a shuffle-board stick on the deck next to him, and he grabbed it.

"What's it look like I'm doing?" cried Artie, rising up and jamming the stick in the wheel.

The boat turned violently, and Shrek lost his balance.

Shrek struggled to his feet and grabbed the wheel, putting the boat back on course. "This really isn't up to you!" he shouted.

Artie stood up and shoved the wheel the other way.

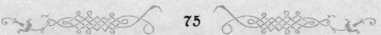

"But I don't know anything about being king," he argued.

"You'll learn on the job!" cried Shrek, as he wrestled to get control of the wheel again.

Donkey and Puss rolled across the deck, shouting.

"Sorry to disappoint you," said Artie, grabbing onto the wheel and pulling hard to the right. "I'm going back!"

"Back to what?" cried Shrek, as he pulled the wheel to the left. "Being a loser?"

But as soon as the words left his lips, Shrek knew he had gone too far. Artie drooped and let go of the wheel. Shrek had been pulling so hard, he yanked the whole steering column from the deck.

"Now look what you did!" he scolded.

Seasick and about to puke, Donkey crawled up to the railing. But right in front of his bleary eyes he could see— rocks! *SHREK!!!*" he shouted.

Desperately, Shrek tried to set the wheel back in place and steer the ship away from the shore.

"Land ho," said the drunken captain, just as the whole boat crashed and splintered against the rocks.

Chapter Thirteen

With Puss under one arm and Donkey under the other, the big ogre stomped out of the water onto shore.

Artie sputtered behind them, pulling himself out of the surf.

Shrek looked over his shoulder and glared at him. "Nice going, Your Highness!"

"Oh, so it's 'Your Highness' again, eh? What happened to 'loser'? Huh?" taunted Artie.

"Hey, if you think this is getting you out of anything, well, it isn't," cried Shrek. "We're heading back to Far Far

 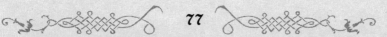

Away, one way or another, and you're gonna be king."

"And you're gonna be king!" mimicked Artie. "Yeah, right." He marched off across the beach and headed for the woods.

"Where do you think you're going!" shouted Shrek.

"Far Far Away . . . from you!" Artie disappeared down a dark path.

"You get back here, young man, and I mean it!" cried Shrek.

Artie didn't respond.

Donkey trotted to catch up to Shrek. "Whoa, hey, Shrek. You're gonna have to change your tactics if you want to get anywhere with this kid," he advised.

Shrek smiled a broad, phony smile. "You're right, Donkey." He picked up a big piece of driftwood. "What about this?" he asked, waving it around like a club.

Donkey shook his head in disgust.

"Oh c'mon. It's just a joke." Shrek laughed and patted Donkey on the head. "Still . . ."

They hurried along a steep, rocky trail through the dark forest, trying to catch up with the reluctant king.

 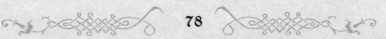

Shrek walked faster. "So . . . Artie . . . listen . . . ," he called, trying to get Artie's attention.

Artie kept his eyes forward, ignoring him.

Shrek moved right up behind him. "Listen, Artie. If you think this whole mad scene ain't dope, I feel you, dude. I mean, I'm not trying to get up in your grill or raise your roof or whatever, but what I am screaming is, yo, check out this ka-zing tha-zing ba-zaby."

Puss and Donkey glanced at each other, confused. Artie spotted smoke in the distance and headed off in that direction, still ignoring the annoying ogre.

"I mean," continued Shrek, "if it doesn't groove or what I'm saying ain't straight trippin,' just say, oh no you didn't, you know, you're getting' on my last nerve. And then I'll know it's . . . then I'll know it's whack, right?"

As Artie passed a tree, he grabbed hold of a branch and let it whack Shrek in the face.

Artie ran toward the plume of smoke. As he emerged from the woods into a little clearing, he saw a big iron pot full of boiling liquid sitting over the campfire in front of a shack built into the hillside.

"Somebody help! I've been kidnapped by a monster!" Artie screamed.

"Artie! Wait!" cried Shrek.

"Help! Help! Help! Felony in progress!" cried Artie.

"Calm down, kid. Jeez," said Shrek.

"C'mon! C'mon! Innocent victim out here! Hello?" Artie called outside the door of the shack.

At that instant, a flash of light shot out of the candle box that hung on the door, and a three-dimensional floating image of an old wizard's head confronted them.

"Ahhhhhhhh!!!" cried Donkey and Puss, clinging to each other in fear.

"ATTENTION, TRESPASSERS!" said the head. "You have disrupted the aura of my serenity circle. Vacate the premises pronto, or prepare to suffer the vengeful wrath of my . . ."

FZZZZZZZZZT. The image suddenly disappeared.

The door of the shack creaked open and a wizened old man stepped out.

"I knew I should have gotten that warranty!" he cried.

 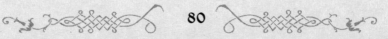

Shrek tries to be a good stand-in king . . .

. . . but he can't seem to get the hang of it!

Shrek and Fiona receive
the royal treatment!

Shrek didn't enjoy the party.

The Frog King is about to croak.

Witness Charming's new profession—
dinner theater fake-ogre dueling.

The queen and the fairy-tale creatures look after the kingdom while Shrek is away.

Charming is up to no good at The Poison Apple.

Shrek visits a distant high school
in search of Artie, the next heir to the throne.

Charming leads his
fairy-tale villains.

Hook terrorizes the citizens of Far Far Away.

Behold the latest trend in baby care—
helper dwarfs.

"Haven't you ever seen a tea party before?"

Shrek and Artie discuss the particulars of being a king.

The princesses are in trouble now. . . .

Charming's high note falls flat when
Shrek takes away his happily-ever-after.

He hit the candle box device with his fist, and it zapped him on the head.

"Ahh! Ow, ow, ow, ow," he cried.

"Mr. Merlin?" asked Artie.

Shrek looked at Artie in surprise. "You know this guy?"

"Yeah. He was the school's magic teacher," said Artie. He leaned closer to Shrek and whispered. "Until he had his nervous breakdown."

"Uh, technically I was merely a victim of a level-three fatigue," Merlin corrected him, "and at the request of my therapist and the school authorities, I have retired to the tranquility of nature to discover my divine purpose."

He swatted at a fly that was trying to land on his head. "Now, can I interest anyone in a snack or beverage? Something to wet your . . . whistle?" Merlin asked, as he whistled a little tune.

"No thanks, my whistle's moist enough as it is," replied Shrek.

Merlin held up a baking dish full of rocks. "Are you

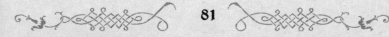

sure you don't want to try my famous *rock au gratin*?" he asked.

"Thanks, but no thanks. We've got a lot of ground to cover," replied Shrek as he grabbed Artie by the arm.

"Who said I was going with you?" said Artie.

"Hey, understand this, kid. There's no more Mr. Nice Guy from here on out," said Shrek.

"So, that was your Mr. Nice Guy?" asked Artie.

"I know, and I'm gonna miss him," quipped Shrek.

"Why don't you go terrorize a village and leave me alone?" asked Artie.

"Oh yeah?" yelled Shrek.

"Yeah!" snapped Artie.

"*Ahhhh! Ahhhhh!* Enough!" shouted Merlin. He got up and threw a handful of dirt in the fire. Plumes of magic smoke rose up into the air.

Everyone stopped bickering and watched.

Merlin scratched his stomach. "Ack! All this blocked denial and renunciation is rashing me up. Look! Look at that!" he cried, lifting his robe so they all could see the rash on his belly.

"Ah!" cried Donkey.

"Dios mio!" meowed Puss.

"You're not going to get anywhere unless you learn to confront your inner demons!" cried Merlin. "Now all of you—look into the smoke and tell me what you see."

Plumes of smoke shot into the air. Different shapes started to form.

"Ooo! Charades!" cried Donkey.

"I see a dirty fire," said Shrek. "Now can we just . . ."

"Oh! I see a Dutch fudge torte with cinnamon swirls!" cried Donkey.

"Looks more like a fiery temptress to me," said Puss.

"Torte," argued Donkey.

"Temptress," insisted Puss.

Merlin turned to Shrek. "Now your turn, monster."

"Forget it," said Shrek.

"C'mon, Shrek!" cried Donkey. "Everybody's doing it!"

"Look, pal, it's either this or some primal scream therapy," said Merlin. "AHHHHHHHHHH!"

"All right! Fine!" growled Shrek.

Merlin tossed another handful of dirt into the fire.

 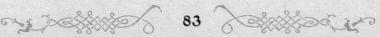

"Tell me what you see!"

As Shrek glanced into the fire, the stroller and baby images from his nightmare on the boat began to take shape in the smoke.

"I see a rainbow pony," said Shrek sarcastically.

"Interesting . . . now the boy!" cried Merlin, pointing to Artie.

Artie squinted at the plumes of smoke. "Okay, I see . . . I don't know . . . some guy . . . and he's standing in front of a castle."

Merlin whacked him on the back of the head. "Stay with it!" he cried.

"Whoa, wait! Now the castle's got teeth! It's chasing him!"

Merlin continued beating a drum. "Maybe he should run?" chimed Merlin.

"Run!" screamed Artie. "No! It just ate me!"

Shrek looked at Artie with growing sympathy.

"Uh . . . I mean, it just ate him," said Artie.

Artie looked up from the fire and noticed everyone staring at him.

"Ahhhhh." Merlin took a deep breath. "My camp is clean again!"

He patted Artie on the shoulder and disappeared inside his shack.

"I know you want me to be king, but I can't. I'm not cut out for it, and I never will be, all right? Even my own dad knew I wasn't worth the trouble. He dumped me at that school the first chance he got, and I never heard from him again," said Artie.

"Look, my dad wasn't really the fatherly type, either," said Shrek sympathetically.

"Well," said Artie, "I doubt he was worse than mine."

"Oh yeah? My father was an ogre. He tried to eat me," Shrek replied.

Artie chuckled. "Okay . . . I guess that's . . . pretty bad."

"I know it's hard to believe with my obvious charm and good looks, but people didn't used to think that much of me either," said Shrek. "And you know what, Artie, just because folks treat you like junk doesn't mean that's what you are."

Donkey and Puss smiled encouragingly at Shrek.

"You just need to do a little less yelling and use a little more soap," added Artie.

Shrek nodded. "Thanks, Artie."

Shrek and Artie, Donkey and Puss sat in a row on the log, staring at the fire.

"The soap's 'cause you stink," explained Artie. "Real bad."

"Yeah. Thanks," said Shrek. "I got that."

Chapter
Fourteen

While Shrek and his friends pondered the frightening idea of fatherhood, Queen Lillian, Fiona, and the other princesses were desperately trying to escape through the secret passageways deep under the castle of Far Far Away. They *had* to find out what the evil Prince Charming was planning!

Fiona was in front, holding a torch to light their way. They tiptoed down a dark stairway and turned a corner onto a narrow ledge.

"Where are we going?" whined Cinderella.

"Just stay close," said Fiona. "There's another entrance into the castle around here somewhere."

Sleeping Beauty yawned. "We've been walking for hours, and my feet are killing me," she complained.

Doris hoisted the drooping Beauty up in her arms and carried her. Before long, Beauty was sound asleep again, her head resting on one of Doris's broad shoulders.

Cinderella sniffed the air. "Oh, this place is filthy. I feel like a hobo."

"Just keep your eyes open," ordered Fiona, trying to hide her frustration. She lowered her torch so the princesses could see the narrowing ledge. A rat scurried across in front of them.

"Ewwwww," cried Snow White.

"Disgusting!" declared Cinderella.

Snow White shuddered. "I'm sorry but this just isn't working for me."

"Everything's always about you, isn't it?" asked Sleeping Beauty, lifting her head from Doris's shoulder. "It's not like your attitude is helping, Snow."

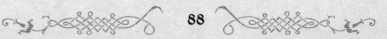

"My attitude!?" cried Snow White. "Well, maybe it just bothers you that I was voted fairest in the land."

"Oh, you mean in that rigged election?" sneered Rapunzel.

"Give me a break! Like you're a natural blonde?" cried Snow, gesturing dramatically at Rapunzel's long tresses. "Oh, Rapunzel, Rapunzel, let down thy golden extensions!"

Queen Lillian interrupted them. "Uh, ladies . . . !"

"Your bickering isn't helping," Fiona declared. "Now, let's go!"

"Hmph," they all grumbled.

Fiona just shook her head and led the way forward.

"So I guess the plan is we just wander aimlessly in this stinky hole until we rot," jeered Snow White.

"No," cried Fiona. "We get inside and find out what Charming's up to."

She searched for the way in. Suddenly she spotted a square of dim light overhead. "That's it!" she cried. She threw down her torch and led the way up a long ladder. She lifted the metal grate and popped her head out into the air.

Fiona crawled out of the hole and into the castle court-yard, with the queen and other princesses behind her.

They snuck around the corner of a building and hid there for a while, watching the strange construction job that was going on. Prince Charming had ordered the building of a big new theater. A large tower façade was hoisted up on the stage, and pictures of Charming were being hung everywhere.

A group of guards marched past, and the princesses hugged the wall.

"Come on, this way!" cried Rapunzel, taking off in the opposite direction.

"Rapunzel, wait!" cried Fiona.

Fiona and the others followed Rapunzel into the castle.

As she charged through the doors, Fiona spotted Prince Charming at the end of the long hallway, holding Rapunzel by the arm.

"Charming, let go of her!" she cried.

Charming smiled his unctuous smile. "Why would I want to do that?"

"Grrrrrrrrrrrrrrrr," Rapunzel purred at him.

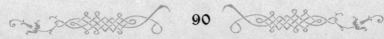

"Woof," he barked at her affectionately, and the two of them shared a long kiss.

The princesses gasped in shock.

"What!?" cried Fiona.

"Say hello, ladies, to the new queen of Far Far Away," declared Prince Charming.

"Jealous much?" asked Rapunzel.

"Rapunzel!" cried Fiona. "How could you!?"

The armed guards moved in and surrounded Queen Lillian and the princesses.

"Thanks to Rapunzel, you'll soon be back where you started," declared Charming, "scrubbing floors or locked away in towers—that is, if I let you last the week!"

"But Pooky, you promised you wouldn't hurt them," Rapunzel whined.

"Not here, Kitten Whiskers," warned Charming. "Daddy will discuss this later."

"Shrek will never let you get away with this, Charming!" cried Fiona.

Prince Charming flashed a sadistic smile. "There's nothing your precious ogre can do to change things this

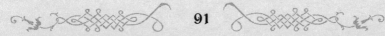

time, princess. Now, forgive us, but we have a show to put on!"

He led Rapunzel out toward the courtyard, and she glanced back at them with a look of apology on her face.

The guards marched off with the defeated princesses in tow.

Chapter
Fifteen

The next morning, Shrek woke up in the deep, dark wood, still lost and far away from Far Far Away. He scratched his head and looked around. Something was amiss, but what was it? He heard a little fluttering sound behind him, and he turned. It was just a little bird landing on the branch of a tree.

As soon as Shrek turned his back again, the branch slammed the little bird against the trunk of the tree, and the bird dropped silently to the ground.

Shrek looked over at Donkey, who was still sound asleep, snoring.

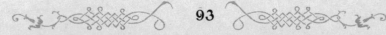

A few leaves drifted down around them, and two long, dark shadows fell across the campsite. Shrek's ogre ears prickled, and a chill went down his spine. He spun around. All around the campsite, trees were moving in!

Puss awoke with a start and leapt onto Shrek's shoulder.

The log Artie was resting on sat up, knocking him to the ground.

"Ugh! Ow!" he cried, springing to his feet.

Before they knew it, evil trees had them surrounded.

Donkey finally began to rouse himself from his slumber.

When he had rubbed the sleep from his eyes, he looked up and saw a horrible tree looming over him.

"Ahhhhhh!!!" he screamed.

Somewhere, off in the woods, piano music was playing.

Shrek peered through the vegetation and spotted Captain Hook at his piano.

"Ha, ha, ha!"

Shrek heard Hook's evil laugh and shivered.

The music built to a pounding crescendo. Finally, Hook looked up from his keys and turned to face them.

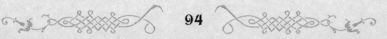

He scowled and barked an order to his pirates: "Kill 'em all!"

He pointed his hook at Shrek malevolently. "Except the fat one. King Charming has something special in mind for you, ogre."

"KING Charming!?" cried Shrek.

"Attack!" ordered Hook.

Pirates dropped from the trees.

One of them raised his sword to swing at Artie. Shrek shoved Artie's head down out of the way, just in the nick of time. The pirate prepared to swing again, and Shrek lifted Artie over his head. Artie aimed with both feet and gave the pirate a powerful kick that sent him tumbling to the ground.

Puss drew his sword and protected Donkey from the pirates who were now swinging down from the branches all around them.

Captain Hook played a rousing fight song on his piano as two pirates wheeled in a large treasure chest.

"Ready the plank!" cried Hook.

A pirate threw a wooden board down on a tree stump.

One end of the board was balanced over the open trunk. Several pirates held Shrek at sword point and forced him to walk the plank into the trunk.

Backs together and swords drawn, Puss, Donkey, and Artie desperately tried holding off the villains. But a net dropped from one of the evil trees and scooped them up. Pirates aimed a cannon at the netted heroes and lit the fuse.

"Ahhhh," cried Artie in a panic.

Puss popped out his claws like switchblades and tried to cut through the netting. Donkey tried gnawing it with his big teeth.

As the fuse burned, Shrek burst out of the treasure chest like a jack-in-the-box. He stood up, with the trunk still stuck to his backside. Spotting the lit fuse, he quickly formulated a plan.

He jumped up and came down hard on one end of the plank. The pirate standing on the other end was catapulted into the air toward the cannon. As the pirate fell on the cannon, it swung around—its barrel now aimed at Captain Hook and his piano!

Kablaaaam! The cannonball shot out and blew the piano to pieces. Hook stared at the wreckage.

Shrek grabbed an ax and threw it at the rope holding the net. The ax cut through the rope and set Artie, Puss, and Donkey free.

The pirates regrouped and started to close in again.

Quickly, Shrek took over the cannon and stuffed in another cannonball.

When the pirates saw the lit fuse, they spun on their heels and retreated into the woods.

"Arrrrr!" cried Captain Hook, shaking his hook in the air. "Cowards!"

Shrek grabbed him. "What has Charming done with Fiona?" he demanded.

"She's going to get what's coming to her!" said Hook. He lifted his hook to strike Shrek, but it caught in the branches of one of the evil trees.

"And there ain't nothing you can do to stop him!" he yelled to Shrek, as the tree dragged him off into the woods, along with the rest of the villains.

Shrek spotted a horse tied to a cart on the far side of

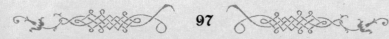

Merlin's camp. "C'mon!" Shrek called to his friends. There was no time to rest. Fiona and the others were in terrible danger!

Shrek just kept going. But Artie darted in front of Shrek and cut him off. "Hold up!" he cried. "Merlin can help you."

Merlin sat cross-legged in front of his hut and began chanting. "I am a flowing river. Flow, flow, flow . . ."

Shrek looked at the old wizard, skeptically. "Oh, I don't think so."

"The guy's a wizard," said Artie. "Are you just going to run all the way home?"

Shrek sighed impatiently. "Oh, all right. You've got one minute! Then we do it my way."

Merlin was still chanting. "I am a buzzing bee. Buzz, buzz, buzz . . ."

"Mr. Merlin!" Artie interrupted him. "We need a spell to get us back to Far Far Away."

Merlin didn't move. He glanced out of the corner of his eye at Artie. "Forget it. I don't have it in me anymore, kid," he said. "I lost most of my good spells years ago in

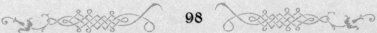

the divorce. That no good, flying fairy sack of bubbles."

Artie sighed.

"I am a flowing river. Flow, flow, flow . . . ," said Merlin, trying to get back into his chant.

"Mr. Merlin . . . ," Artie tried again. "Please. I know you can do it."

"I said, forget it!" shouted Merlin.

Artie paused, thought for a moment, and then burst into tears.

Merlin looked at him. "What's with you?"

"It's just so hard," sobbed Artie. "We really need to get back, 'cause the kingdom's in trouble, 'cause there's a really bad man, and it's just so hard. . . ."

"C'mon, take it easy." Merlin stood up and moved closer to him.

"I don't think you understand," Artie blubbered. "There's a mean person doing mean things to good people, and . . ."

"Maybe you should sit down," said Merlin, growing more and more uncomfortable.

Artie grabbed Merlin, pleading desperately, ". . . and

XV

they really need your help to get them back! Why won't you help them? Tell me!"

"Have a heart, old man," added Shrek for good measure.

Merlin was speechless.

"Pleeeease," Artie begged.

What could Merlin do!? "Uh . . . ok . . . I'll go get my things," he said, helplessly.

As Merlin slipped into his shack, Artie recovered instantly. He looked at Shrek and shrugged. "Piece of cake."

Shrek smiled at him, pleased with his performance.

Merlin returned with his spell book. "Now, I'm a bit rusty," he warned, "so there may be some side effects."

"Side effects?" cried Donkey.

"Don't worry, whatever it is, or no matter how excruciatingly painful it may be, it'll wear off eventually . . . I think." Merlin prepared to begin. He stretched his arms and cracked his knuckles. As he did, a bolt of lightning shot out of his fingertips and shattered a rock nearby.

"Ah!" cried Donkey.

"Oops," said Merlin.

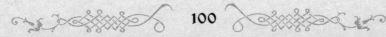

He began chanting again.

"Are you sure this is a good idea?" whined Donkey, shooting Shrek a worried look.

Shrek pointed to Merlin. "On with the whammy-zammy."

Donkey and Puss cowered.

"Alacritious-expeditious-a-zoomy-zoom-zoom. Let's help our friends get back . . . uh . . . soon!" said Merlin, uncertainly.

Magic rays shot from Merlin's extended fingers, and Shrek, Puss, Donkey, and Artie disappeared in a puff of smoke.

"Whoa!" cried Merlin, blowing the smoke from his fingertips. "It worked! Nice kids."

Chapter
Sixteen

In a flash, the "kids" found themselves falling from the sky. They bounced down through the branches of an apple tree and landed, all in a heap, at the base of the tree.

Donkey moaned and groaned and shifted his poor body, trying to get comfortable. "Oh, man, I haven't been on a trip like that since college."

Shrek's jaw dropped. Was that Donkey's voice coming out of Puss's mouth? "Donkey!?" he cried.

"What? Is there something in my teeth?" Donkey looked down at his body, and his eyes widened in shock.

"Huh!? What the—? Oh no!" he cried. "I've been abra-cadabra'd into a fancy-feasting, second-rate sidekick."

"Actually, I think you look quite handsome," said Puss from Donkey's body. "I am the one who looks like some bloated roadside piñata."

"Uh, sorry about that, guys," Artie apologized.

"Don't be!" cried Shrek. "You got us back, kid. Thanks." He pointed to a castle on the hillside, just a few miles away. It was the castle of Far Far Away! He helped Artie off the ground, and the four friends hurried off.

As they entered the city, they saw the destruction that Charming and his villains left behind. The welcome sign had been boarded over. Instead of FAR FAR AWAY it now read GO GO AWAY.

Poor Donkey's new feet were hurting in Puss's wee little boots. "Seriously," he complained, paying no attention to the sign, "how in the Hans Christian Andersen am I supposed to parade around in these goofy boots!? Man, you need some comfort inserts or arch supports or something . . ."

Suddenly the view of the city before them hit Donkey

like a ton of bricks. "Whoa!" he cried.

The whole place looked like a war zone. Fires burned in the street, carriages were up on cinder blocks with their wheels missing, and there was graffiti everywhere.

They made a wide circle around a drunken pirate passed out on the curb.

"So this is the cesspool you want me to be king of?" questioned Artie.

"It wasn't like this when we left," said Shrek.

Suddenly, he spotted a little marionette theater. Dancing inside it, behind the glass window was . . . Who? He squinted in disbelief. "Pinocchio?" he called.

"Shrek!" shouted the little puppet.

As Shrek and the others rushed toward the theater, the curtains began to close. Pinocchio pressed his hands against the glass.

"Pinocchio!" cried Shrek.

"Shrek!"

"Pinocchio!"

"Help me," squeaked the puppet.

"What's happened?" asked Shrek.

"Charming and the villains have taken over everything!" cried Pinocchio. "They attacked us, but Fiona and the princesses got away. Now she's . . ."

The music wound down and the curtains closed on the little theater, blocking the window completely.

"She's what!? She's what!?" cried Shrek. He pulled out his wallet and shook it upside down, desperately searching for some money. Nothing.

He looked at Artie.

Artie turned his pockets inside out and shrugged.

Shrek turned to Puss in Donkey's body. "Puss, loan me five bucks!"

"C'mon, Puss, you heard the man. Help a brother out," cried Donkey from Puss's body.

"Do you see any pockets on me?" asked Puss, looking at his donkey body in disgust.

"Hold on a second," said Donkey. He reached down and pulled off one of Puss's fine Corinthian leather boots and turned it upside down. A bag of coins fell to the ground. "A-ha!" he cried, tossing the bag to Shrek.

"I was saving that for the hungry orphans of Sister

Santa Maria's Home for Wayward Youths, but I'm sure they'll understand," explained Puss.

Shrek quickly began putting coins in the machine. The music revved up, the curtain came up, and the stringed puppet danced once again.

"Quick, Pinocchio. Where is Fiona?" asked Shrek.

"Charming's got her locked away someplace secret," squeaked Pinocchio. "You gotta find him! He's probably getting ready for the showwwwwwww. . . ."

The curtain went down.

"Wait, wait, wait!" cried Shrek. "Pinocchio! What show?"

Pinocchio's little puppet hand reached out from under the curtain and pointed to the poster on the wall of a building nearby.

The picture on the poster showed Prince Charming, sword raised in the air, with his foot pinning Shrek to the ground.

"It's a Happily Ever-After, After All!" Shrek read. "One Night Only at the Castle. History the Way It Was Meant to Be."

"Whoa, Shrek!" cried Donkey. "You didn't tell us you were in a play."

"Well, I guess I've been so busy I forgot to mention it," quipped Shrek.

Suddenly they heard a voice from the courtyard shouting: "It's the ogre! Get him!"

Shrek turned and saw a group of royal knights armed and ready. He put on his most princely manner and strode toward them. "Look, I don't know who dropped the ball on this one, but the carriage was supposed to pick me up at my hotel," he declared. "Donkey," he said to Puss, "we're dealing with amateurs."

The knights exchanged confused looks.

Artie tore the poster off the wall and confronted them. "Do you know who this is?" he demanded. He turned to Shrek with an apologetic look. "I am so sorry about this, sir."

"Just take care of it," commanded Shrek. "And quickly!"

Artie turned and addressed the leaders. "I assume you have everything ready for tonight! You did get the list for the dressing room, didn't you?"

Donkey, in Puss's body, marched up to the two in charge and eyed them. "Yeah, the breakfast croissants stuffed with seared sashimi tuna," he added imperiously. "The vanilla crepes with orange sauce, the chilled fruit soup. Oh, and please tell me you at least have the saffron corn with the jalapeño honey butter, 'cause our client cannot get into his proper emotional state without his jalapeño honey butter."

"Uh . . . ," the first knight stammered.

"I don't think that's our department," dithered the other.

Shrek shoved them aside and strode toward the castle.

Donkey, with Puss's fiercest eyes, glared over his shoulder at the nervous knights. "Looks like we're gonna have to inform Charming he's got a couple of boobs running the operation."

Chapter
Seventeen

Prince Charming's stagehands were busy building the set for the evening's performance. Charming and Cyclops, in tuxedoes and top hats, were rehearsing a little dance number, along with an ensemble of witches and dwarfs.

"Wink and turn, and wink and turn, and wink and . . . jazz hands!" directed Charming.

Eager to please, Cyclops grabbed his hat and flung out his hands, smacking Charming right in the face with his hat.

"No, you fat-eyed klutz!" cried Charming. "It's shuffle, shuffle, shuffle—cha, cha, cha!"

While Charming fumed in frustration, Rapunzel stormed up to him clutching a cheesy red-sequined dress.

"You expect me to wear this?" she demanded.

"It was Mother's evening gown," said Prince Charming.

"Ugh," cried Rapunzel, repulsed.

"One time, for my 'happily-ever-after'?" oozed Charming.

"We need to talk," declared Rapunzel.

"Not now, darling," replied Charming. "I'm up to my ears in this show. We can talk after I defeat the monster and rescue you from your tower."

Rapunzel flung the dress on the stage floor and stomped out.

Charming called to her halfheartedly. "Oh, c'mon, pumpkin."

"Freak!" cried Rapunzel, slamming the door behind her.

Charming glared at the dancers. "Who told you to stop dancing!?"

"Uh . . . wink and turn, wink and turn . . . ," repeated poor Cyclops, clomping out the steps.

Prince Charming locked himself up in his new gold-plated dressing room and sulked. The walls were covered with portraits of himself in a variety of acting roles. He plopped down on the throne in front of his dressing table and stared at his own face in the three-sided mirror. He sighed and adjusted the angle for a better view. But there behind him, standing in the doorway was—Shrek! Artie, Donkey, and Puss stood beside him.

Charming turned to them.

"It's over, Charming," said Shrek, looming toward him.

Charming backed up against his dressing table.

"So glad you could make it back," he said nonchalantly. "I was afraid you might miss the show." He fumbled around behind his back for a moment and pushed a hidden button under the tabletop.

Shrek picked him up by his shirtfront and scowled. "Where's Fiona?" he demanded.

"Don't worry," sneered Charming. "She and the others are safe. For now."

Shrek tightened his grip, thinking he might just wring

this schemer's neck! But at that moment a group of guards burst into the room and surrounded them.

A knight arrived behind them, carrying a basket of fruit. "Well, I hope this makes up for any misunderstanding," he apologized.

Charming looked at him, confused.

Seeing the situation, the knight backed quickly out of the room and vanished.

Charming smiled. "I think it's best you let me go," he said to the ogre.

The guards were all pointing their swords directly at Shrek. He dropped Charming to the floor with a thud.

Charming got back on his feet and brushed himself off.

Artie struggled past the guards and glared at Charming. "You're not the true king of Far Far Away!"

Charming rolled his eyes and strolled over to Artie. "And you are, I suppose?" he asked, laughing.

Artie stuck out his chin valiantly. "Yeah."

Charming chuckled and raised his eyebrows at Shrek. "This boy is supposed to be the new king of Far

 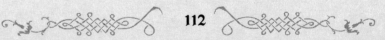

Far Away? How pathetic," said Charming as he looked Artie up and down.

"That's enough, Charming. I'm here now, you got what you wanted. This isn't about him. Go, Artie," cried Shrek. "This isn't about you."

"Then who is it about? I'm supposed to be king, right?" asked Artie.

"You weren't really next in line for the throne," said Shrek.

"But you said the king asked for me personally," declared Artie.

"Not exactly," said Shrek.

Artie looked at Puss and Donkey, hoping for some kind of explanation. But they quickly looked away.

"But you said . . ."

"I said whatever I had to say, all right? I wasn't right for the job and I needed some fool to replace me, and you fit the bill. So just go!"

Artie slumped. "You've been playing me the whole time," he declared.

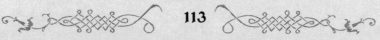

At that, Prince Charming motioned to the guards to let Artie go.

Artie walked toward the door, but then stopped and looked back at Shrek.

"Just leave!" cried Shrek.

As Shrek hung his head in shame, Charming leaned in close to taunt him. "You really have a way with children, Shrek."

Charming motioned to the guards to take the ogre and his sidekicks away.

Chapter Eighteen

Locked away in the dark dungeon, the princesses were going stir crazy. "Gotta clean, gotta clean, gotta clean," repeated Cinderella, polishing every filthy thing in sight. "Gotta clean, gotta keep it clean. Gotta keep it clean. Bright and shiny kittens . . ."

Sleeping Beauty lay snoring on an old prison cot. Snow White was pacing the damp concrete floor. Doris tried to pry the prison bars apart with the sheer force of her enormous arms, until something cracked in her back.

Fiona stared out the narrow window toward the castle.

Snow White complained as she paced. "Had we just

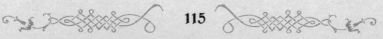

stayed put like I suggested, we could be sipping tea out of little heart-shaped cups."

"Yeah, yeah, heart-shaped cups," Cinderella agreed.

"Eating crumpets smothered with loganberries," continued Snow White.

"Yeah, loganberries," echoed Cinderella.

"Stop it, Cindy," cried Snow White.

"Yeah, just stop talking." repeated Cinderella. She stared crazily at her own reflection in a puddle on the floor.

"Who cares who's running the kingdom, anyway?" declared Snow White.

"I care," said Fiona.

She and Queen Lillian stepped forward. "And you should all care, too," said the queen.

At that moment the door of their prison cell flew open, and a guard tossed Donkey and Puss in with them.

"Hey, hey, hey," cried Puss in Donkey's body. He glared indignantly at the manhandling guard.

"Yeah," agreed Donkey in Puss's body, "and can I have your badge number, 'Tin Can'—"

The door clanked shut behind them.

"Donkey!?" cried Fiona.

"Princess!?" cried Donkey.

"Puss??" asked Fiona.

Puss waved his donkey hoof. "*Lo siento*, Princesa, but I am Puss, stuck here inside this hideous body."

"And I'm me!" cried Donkey, waving his kitty paw.

Fiona looked from one to the other, confused. "But you're . . ."

"I know, I know," said Donkey. "Everything's a little fruity in the loops right now. But what happened is, we went to high school, the boat crashed, and we got 'bippity-boppity-booped' by the Magic Man."

"You poor, sweet things," purred Doris.

"I don't get it," cried Cinderella.

"The cat turned into a little horse that smells like feet," explained Snow White. "What's to get?"

"Huh? Who's that?" asked Sleeping Beauty, half-waking from her doze.

"Where's Shrek?" asked Fiona.

"Charming's got him," said Donkey. "And he plans

 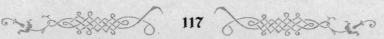

on taking care of Shrek tonight in front of the whole kingdom."

Fiona and her mother exchanged worried glances.

Fiona took a deep breath. "All right everyone, we need to find a way out, now."

"Yes, yes. You're right," the princesses mumbled in agreement.

"Ladies, assume the position!" cried Snow White.

At that, Sleeping Beauty lay down as if asleep, Cinderella dusted off a spot and sat down, and Snow White lay back on a cot with her lips puckered.

"What in the world are you doing?" asked Fiona.

"Waiting to be rescued," explained Sleeping Beauty.

"You have got to be kidding me," cried Fiona.

"Well, what do you expect us to do?" asked Snow White. "We're just four . . . ," she considered Doris for a moment, " . . . I mean three super-hot princesses, three circus freaks, a pregnant ogre, and an old lady."

Queen Lillian smiled and casually walked past the princesses. "Excuse me. Old lady coming through." She moved up to the cell wall, laid her hands against it, yelled

"Hiiiiiiiiiiiyyyyyyyyiiiiiiaaaaaaaahhhh!!!" and head-butted a hole right through the bricks!

"Whoa," cried the princesses, impressed.

"Oh, look," said the queen. "I've stumbled across an opening."

"Mom?" gasped Fiona.

"Well, you didn't actually think you got your fighting skills from your father, did you?" she asked.

Fiona beamed proudly at her mom. She turned to the princesses with renewed confidence. "Okay girls, from here on out, we're gonna take care of business ourselves."

The princesses watched her intently.

"So, why didn't she just bust through the wall earlier?" asked Snow White.

"Do you want your happily-ever-after back or not?" insisted Fiona.

Snow White thought about it for a moment. She glanced over at the other princesses. They all nodded.

With determined looks the princesses prepared for battle. Snow ripped off her sleeve to reveal a tattoo—of a dwarf. Sleeping Beauty tore off the hem of her frilly dress

and Queen Lillian put antiglare smudges under her eyes with lipstick, while Cinderella sharpened the heel of her glass slipper.

The princesses got into a huddle and put their hands together in solidarity. Puss and Donkey added their paws, too. "Let's go!" they cheered. It was time for them to save the kingdom!

Chapter
Nineteen

The prisoners escaped from their cell and headed toward the castle. Fiona could see two evil trees guarding the entrance. She signaled Snow White with a duck call. Snow brushed off her skirt, tidied her hair, and skipped innocently down the path by herself. She stopped in front of the evil trees, singing prettily: *"Ha ha ha ha haaaaa. Little birdies take a wink, flitting down from the trees, they appear and chirp in my ear."*

Soon all the little forest creatures were flocking to Snow White.

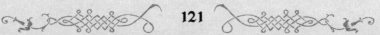

"Watch the hair," she cautioned, not missing a beat. *"All because I sing. Ahh ha ha ha ha haaa."*

The evil trees stared in delight as more and more creatures gathered around the beautiful princess.

"Ahh ha ha ha ha haaaa," she continued, until all the animals had arrived. Then her whole face changed in an instant. With the eye of the tiger, she turned to the animals and her song switched from sweet to tough. *"Ahhaha!! Ahhaha!!!"*

As if on command, the animals began to attack the evil trees. While the trees were busy fighting off the feisty furballs, Fiona led the charge of princesses. "Move it! Go! Go! Go!" she commanded.

Puss and Donkey took off in their own direction. They ran through the front gates of the Far Far Away Zoo, where the Dronkeys were being held captive.

"My babies!" cried Donkey from Puss's body. He burst open their cage. Not knowing their dad was in the cat's body, the Dronkeys swarmed over to Puss and hugged his donkey form.

"Ow, help!" Puss screamed.

* * *

The princesses, however, ran toward the castle entrance. Doris punched through the lock and opened the gate. As the princesses entered the castle grounds, a group of guards approached them.

Cinderella aimed her glass slipper at one of them. It knocked him out cold and came swooping back to her hand like a boomerang. Sleeping Beauty fell to the ground, and the guards stumbled and tripped over her. With the guards in chaos and confusion, Doris gave the princesses a leg up over the castle wall.

Downtown, Donkey and Puss raced toward the little puppet theater, where Charming was holding Pinocchio captive. They smashed the glass front of the theater and pulled Pinocchio out.

Gingy was locked up in a display case at the local bakery. He spotted his friends outside and banged on the glass. Donkey, in Puss's body, rushed into the bakery and tried to cut a hole in the glass with his claws. Puss, in Donkey's body, figured out an easier way. He

smashed the glass with his hoof, and Donkey pulled little Gingy out.

"Let's do this thing, people," Donkey shouted as he marched in Puss's boots. "Go Team Dy-No-Mite!"

"Um, Donkey, sir," Pinocchio said. "I thought we agreed to go by the name Team Super Cool."

"As I recall it was Team Awesome," Gingy stated.

"I voted for Team Alpha Wolf Squadron!" Wolf complained.

"All right, all right, all right!" Donkey groaned. "From now on we'll be known as Team Alpha Super Awesome Cool Dy-No-Mite Wolf Squadron!"

On the way back to the castle, one of the Three Little Pigs noticed someone staring at them from behind the bushes. It was Artie! As soon as Puss and Donkey started to approach him, he turned away from them.

"You both knew what was going on the whole time and you kept it to yourselves," said Artie.

"Artie, Shrek only said those things to protect you!" said Puss.

Artie stopped to think about it.

"Shrek saved your life!" cried Donkey.

Artie thought for a moment and suddenly came to a realization.

Chapter
Twenty

Prince Charming's stage was elaborately set up. Captain Hook was conducting the orchestra. He tapped his metal appendage on the music stand to get their attention.

The people of Far Far Away were taking their seats. The lights dimmed, and spotlights crisscrossed the audience. The curtain came up, and smoke billowed across the stage like fog. It came to a stop below a tower.

A spotlight shone on Rapunzel in the tower window, and she began singing: *"I wait alone up here. I'm*

trapped another day. Locked up here—please set me free. My new life I almost see. A castle, you, and me. Yes, a castle, you, and me . . ."

Then, from underneath the stage, a clamshell rose up and opened, revealing Prince Charming on horseback.

"'Tis I! 'Tis I!" he cried. "Upon my royal steed! Princess, my love, at last you shall be freed!"

Rose petals floated down onto the stage like pink snow, and Charming and his steed leapt out of the clamshell.

As he made his way to the tower, Charming sang, "I'm strong and brave, and dashing my way there! With speed! With might! With soft and bouncy hair! Through the blistering desert!"

Charming swung his sword and chopped the head off a griffin puppet.

"Hot!" chorused the evil trees.

"Across the stormiest sea!" Charming dismounted with a flourish and easily swooped the head off a card-board sea serpent.

"Wet!" chorused the evil dwarfs.

"Facing the fiercest of fanged fiends!" he sang, cutting the heads off a wooden bear and reindeer.

"Foul!" chorused the fairy-tale villains.

"So you can gaze upon me-me-me-me-ME!" Charming stood under Rapunzel's tower, serenading her.

"I knew you'd come for me," she sang in reply. *"And now we finally meet."*

"I knew you'd wait. And from my plate of love you'd eat," sang Charming.

Rapunzel let down her long braid.

From the loudspeakers came a growling sound. A trapdoor onstage burst open in a flash of light and smoke.

Charming couldn't resist hamming it up. He put his hand to his ear to listen and widened his eyes in mock surprise. Backstage, Mabel roared into a megaphone and evil dwarfs turned a big metal lever.

As they cranked, a large imposing shadow fell across the stage.

The audience oooo'd and *ahhhhh*'d as the big ogre rose up through the trapdoor, gruesomely lit from below.

"Who is this terrible, ugly fiend who so rudely

intervened?" cried Charming.

"Will Charming fight? Or will he flee?" sang the fairy-tale villains, while pirates and evil knights danced in the background.

"Oh, please rescue me!" sang Rapunzel.

"From this monstrosity!" chorused the villains.

Charming struck a dramatic pose. *"Fear thee not, mademoiselle! I will send this thing back to HELL!"* he sang.

Shrek's eyes widened in amazement, as Charming's voice stretched to hit the ultrahigh notes.

Charming pulled out his sword and aimed it at the ogre's chest. His voice climbed even higher as he sang. *"And you are about to enter a world of pain with which you are not—familiaAAAAAR!!"*

As he held the last high note, glass goblets began to shatter.

"Ha!" he cried triumphantly.

"It can't be any more painful than your singing," quipped Shrek.

The audience roared with laughter. Charming froze,

distracted. He tried to remember his next line. He cued Captain Hook to start the music again.

"Prepare, foul beast, your time is done," he sang.

"Oh, please not again," moaned Shrek. "Have mercy. Kill me first."

The crowd began to laugh again, and Shrek smiled, pleased at the effect he was having on the audience.

Charming fumed. "Stop it! You're ruining the show!"

"Stop it! You're ruining the show!" Shrek mimicked.

"Cut that out!"

"Cut that out!"

"I mean it!!"

"I mean it!!"

Charming raised his sword and pointed it in Shrek's face. "ENOUGH!" he commanded.

The crowd hushed.

Charming drew back his sword, ready to strike. "Now you'll finally know what it is like to have everything you worked for, everything that's precious to you taken away. Now you'll know how I felt." He clenched his teeth and

thrust with all his might.

The audience gasped.

Then ...

Suddenly, a fireball spread across the sky as Dragon flew above the theater, melting Charming's sword.

"Achtung!" cried one of the Three Little Pigs, as he and his brothers flew across the stage on the headless griffin.

Little Pinocchio flew in on his strings. And Gingy popped out of a bag of popcorn in the audience and jumped onto the stage. The Wolf unzipped his wolf costume and stepped out.

With a great roar overhead, Dragon flew by, with Puss and Donkey riding, and the little Dronkeys following close behind.

"Pray for mercy from Puss!" shouted Puss in Donkey's body.

"And Donkey!" Donkey hissed from Puss's body.

And then the queen broke through the backdrop with a giant head-butt, followed by Sleeping Beauty and Doris.

 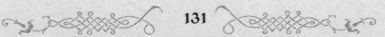

Snow White flew in behind them, and Cinderella ran on stage holding a mop as a weapon. The princesses struck a pose next to Shrek as the audience burst into applause. Suddenly, the front door of the "swamp house" onstage crashed to the floor, revealing Fiona!

"Hi, honey! Are we late?"

"Just in time," declared Shrek.

Charming clapped his hands at the orchestra and nodded to Captain Hook.

The fairy-tale villains suddenly realized that this was their summons. One by one they moved to take action. Cyclops emerged from a trapdoor, cornering Donkey and Puss. The witches flew in to surround all of the princesses, and Gingy was surrounded by evil knights. There was no way out!

With a dramatic sweep of his sword, Prince Charming ordered the villains to attack!

Suddenly, a powerful spotlight shone into Charming's face. When Shrek looked up, he saw Artie in the rafters above.

Artie jumped down from the rafters and addressed the crowd onstage and the audience. "Who really thinks we need to settle things this way?"

The villains' hands shot up into the air.

"You're really telling me you just want to be villains your whole life?" Artie demanded.

The villains loomed closer.

"But we are villains," offered Hook. "It's the only thing we know."

"But didn't you ever wish you could be something else?" asked Artie.

The villains looked at each other and considered the question.

"Well, it's easy for you to say," piped one of the evil trees. "You're not some evil, enchanted tree."

Prince Charming growled in frustration. "You idiots!" he shouted. "Don't listen to him! Attack them!"

Another evil tree reached around Charming from behind and put a branch over his mouth.

"What Steve's saying here, is that it's hard to come by

honest work when the whole world's against you," explained another tree.

"Right, thanks, Ed," said the first.

Artie walked among the villains, looking each one in the eye. "Fair enough," he said.

The fairy-tale villains sighed and murmured among themselves in agreement.

"A good friend of mine once told me just because people treat you like a villain doesn't mean you are one."

The fairy-tale villains listened intently.

"The thing that matters most is what you think of yourself," Artie added. "If there's something you really want to be, then the only person standing in your way is you."

Artie glanced over at Shrek and they exchanged smiles.

A pirate looked alarmed. "Me?" he cried.

"No, no, no! What I mean is that each of you is standing in your own way!" Artie yelled.

By now the villains were all nodding in agreement.

 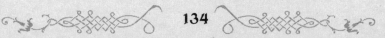

The Headless Horseman pushed through the crowd. "I've always wanted to learn to play guitar," he confessed.

"I'd like to open a spa in France," said the Evil Queen.

"I grow daffodils," said Captain Hook.

Everyone stared at the crusty old pirate in disbelief.

"And they are beautiful!" he added.

One by one the villains threw down their weapons and began chatting with one another about their hopes and dreams.

Prince Charming looked on, stunned. His army had disarmed! Angrily he kicked himself free of the tree and grabbed a discarded sword. He gritted his teeth and charged through the crowd toward Artie, shouting, *"Aaaaaaaahhhhhhhhh!!!"*

Artie faced him bravely. Shrek saw what was happening and, using all of his strength, he managed to break the chains holding him. Shrek flung the chain at Charming's sword and yanked the villain around. Charming kept charging and ran his sword right into Shrek.

The ogre fell to his knees as everyone stood by in

horror. Prince Charming couldn't believe his eyes — he'd finally killed his worst enemy.

Shrek turned to Artie. "Was that convincing enough?" he asked. Shrek laughed as he revealed the sword safely nestled between his arm and side.

"This was supposed to be *my* happily-ever-after!" Charming shouted.

"Well, I guess you need to keep looking . . . because I'm not giving up mine!" responded Shrek.

And with that, Shrek summoned Dragon to tip the tower over with her tail. Charming looked up as the set fell upon him.

When the dust cleared, Artie leaned down to pick up the crown that had tumbled off Charming's head. He looked at it closely.

"It's yours if you want it, you know," said Shrek.

Artie looked up and saw Shrek smiling at him.

"But this time it's your choice," Shrek added.

Artie smiled back. He was about to answer, when all the villains and fairy-tale creatures joined together and

lifted him up over their shoulders. "Ar-tie! Ar-tie! Ar-tie!" they cheered.

What could he do!? Artie shrugged and put on the crown.

Donkey fought back the tears. "Ah man, just look at him. Our boy's all grown up."

"Yes. We have done well, my friend," said Puss.

"You know what, Puss," said Donkey, "once I got used to doing my business in a box of sand, and I finally gave in to the urge give myself one of your 'cat baths' . . ."

"Please say you didn't!" cried Puss.

"I realized being a cat is okay."

"And once my nose was numb to the stink of your hide, I realized donkeys are strong, loyal, and trustworthy," confessed Puss.

"Friends forever," cried Donkey.

"*Si*," agreed Puss.

Suddenly, Merlin appeared in a puff of smoke. Puss and Donkey approached him.

"Okay, señor hocus-y pocus-y. The time has come to

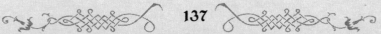

rectify some wrongs!" cried Puss.

"Yes, 'cause I'm not doing anymore of these cat baths," said Donkey.

Merlin rubbed his hands together. "You may feel a pinch," he said.

Bolts of lightning shot out of his magic fingers, and instantly Puss and Donkey were switched back into their own bodies.

"Ooo! I'm me again!" cried Donkey.

"And I am *not* you!" cheered Puss.

The two pals hugged each other again and laughed and walked away.

Merlin chuckled as he saw that Puss still had Donkey's tail, and Donkey still had Puss's tail. "Ah, never mind," Merlin said as he slipped away.

Fiona glanced over at her mother and smiled. Queen Lillian nodded and smiled back.

Shrek took Fiona's hand. "Sorry I left you here," he said. "I should never have gone."

"For what it's worth, I think you would have made a great king," said Fiona.

"I have something more important in mind," said Shrek. He smiled and touched her belly.

Fiona smiled, and the ogre and wife shared a long, smoochy kiss.

Chapter
Twenty-One

Fiona and Shrek returned happily to their swamp, and it wasn't long before their home was filled by the pitter-patter of little ogre feet.

Shrek was the expert at making baby formula from slug juice, eyeballs, and worms. He filled the gourd bottles and carried them over to Fiona, who was sitting in the comfy chair by the fireplace. She held two babies on her lap, and another crawled over to Shrek and tugged at his leg. Shrek laughed and gave Fiona and the babies a big hug.

After feeding time, Donkey and Puss showed up at the ogres' door.

"Hey! I smell Shrek, Jr.!" cried Donkey. Dronkeys streamed in behind him as he entered. Dragon peered in fondly from the doorway.

Shrek did his best trying to change the babies. He twisted the diaper around, gave it a tug, and the baby went flying through the air, landing in a diaper that Fiona was holding.

Puss looked down at one of the ogre triplets on the floor. The baby pulled the pacifier out of her mouth, shoved it into Puss's, and gave Puss a hug, while a Dronkey baby pulled on Puss's tail.

"Peek-a-boo!" called Donkey, covering his eyes with his big ears. The little ones squealed in delight.

One of the ogre babies pulled the wax out of Daddy's ear and began using it like a crayon to draw pictures.

Bursting with pride, Queen Lillian bounced one of her grandbabies on her lap.

Suddenly they heard a knock at the door.

Donkey was lying back on the floor holding one of the gourd bottles in his hooves and drinking from it. Shrek grabbed the bottle from Donkey on his way to the door.

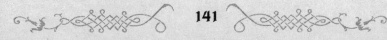

"Hey," Donkey complained.

Shrek opened the door, and there stood the nanny dwarf Snow White had given them.

"Where's the baby?" demanded the dwarf.

Shrek popped the bottle in the dwarf's mouth and shooed him away. He and Fiona were going to do this parenting thing themselves!

Indoors and out, the swamp was overrun by bouncing babies. Shrek built them a beautiful mud slide. Then came Shrek himself, with the most enormous *sploosh*! The little ones giggled in glee.

In the evening, all bathed and diapered and fed, the babies were almost ready to go to sleep. Shrek held one baby over his shoulder and burped him. Fiona patted and burped another. The third crawled past one of the Dronkeys, who let out a little flame belch of his own, lighting the ogre baby's fart like a flame thrower.

Fiona and Shrek looked on proudly. They gathered up the babies and tucked them in.

"Finally," sighed Shrek. For the first time all day,

the swamp was as quiet as a church. "Well, what shall we do now?"

Before they could move an inch, they were both fast asleep. Until ...

"*Waaaaaaaaaaaaaaaa!*"

"Ugh ... Shrek," Fiona sighed.

"I'm on it," he muttered, as he stumbled to the kitchen to warm up the gourds of yummy slug juice.

Soon all the babies were drinking from their bottles contentedly. Shrek beamed as he watched them through his sleepy ogre eyes. And he knew it was really true. He had found what he was looking for—his happily-ever-after, after all!